A HANK OF HAIR

Charlotte Jay was born in 1919 in Adelaide. She spent decades travelling, living and writing in England, Europe, Asia, the Middle East and the Pacific. The famous American critic Dorothy B. Hughes has described her as 'one of the most important writers of far-off places and their mysterious qualities'. She died in 1996 in Adelaide.

BEAT NOT THE BONES

ARMS FOR ADONIS

A HANK of HAIR

A CHARLOTTE JAY NOVEL

Wakefield
Press

Wakefield Press
16 Rose Street
Mile End
South Australia 5031
www.wakefieldpress.com.au

First published by William Heinemann, London, and
Harper and Row, New York, 1964
Revised edition published in Wakefield Crime Classics November 1992
This edition published 2019

Edited by Jane Arms
Designed by Liz Nicholson, Wakefield Press

ISBN 978 1 74305 681 3

A catalogue record for this
book is available from the
National Library of Australia

Wakefield Press thanks
Coriole Vineyards for
continued support

For David and Jonathon Halls

CHAPTER 1

I'm not going to give explanations and make excuses. I'll tell you what happened, and you can draw your own conclusions.

You might say that I had too much time on my hands. Time for those luxuries of the human heart – hatred, dread and grief – and a life so empty there was virtually nothing that had to be moved out of the way when they entered to inhabit it. Time – that precious boon, so we are told. Ironically, it was given to me by my wife.

She had a considerable private income. When she was alive I never saw any of it, having taken a romantic stand about not touching a woman's money, keeping my self-respect, being the dominant male, and all that goes with that. I was a silly little man. Only once in my life have I ceased to be a silly little man . . . But when she died it came to me, and as there was no one around then to applaud the part I was playing – no one at all – well, I just gave up work and lived off it.

And with the full approbation of my doctor. Perhaps he thought he was being original. Not for him the customary clichés about not giving yourself time to think and burying your grief under a pile of work. He seemed to think I was made of stouter stuff. He was a bit of a philosopher really; he had mistaken his vocation. Go away and come to terms with your own sorrow, was his advice. Travel, he said, go right away . . . So that's what I did. I travelled thirty miles up to London, which wasn't exactly what he had in mind.

I had leisure. So had Doyle, I believe. I don't know how he got his, perhaps he inherited it too, or perhaps he robbed a bank. I don't know. I still don't know very much about him, in spite of our comradeship. But it's my belief that he never had to work, not in any real sense. He was quite undisciplined. Work reduces a man, tames him.

You're looking impatient. I'm rambling. And in any case you think my judgement is biased. I'll get to the point.

You remember the wreck off the coast of Spain? A Greek and Norwegian ship ran into one another in heavy fog. A hundred lives were lost – my wife, Rachel, among them. So there I was, Gilbert Hand, forty-three and a widower.

Rachel was two years younger than I was, and when I first met her she was on the way to making a name for herself as a commercial artist. Really she was only playing at it, keeping herself busy until some man came along. There was all that money, you see. After we married she dropped her blossoming career without regret, settled herself into our house in Surrey and busied herself with a dog, a cat, the garden and village affairs. We had no children, which disappointed her, but she soon accepted it. She was happy and uncomplaining. Her whole appearance – her soft, rather full figure, her broad pale face – spelled contentment. Her eyes were large and heavy lidded, her glossy and abundant brown hair drawn back into a thick knot at the nape of her neck – it was beautiful.

The ten years of our marriage were happy and so peaceful that after a year or two I almost forgot I loved her. But I never looked at another woman. This may surprise you, but I have always looked on myself as having a rather tepid sexual drive.

I had a job as a junior partner in a firm that combined bookselling with a little esoteric publishing. It was not very lucrative, but we were well enough off because, though I didn't touch Rachel's money, she did.

I became very wrapped up in the work and spent a good deal of time away from Rachel. It seems to me now that I neglected her shamelessly.

Why? I ask myself now. The silly little books we published, the worthless books we sold. Timid and safe, that was what I was, until Rachel died. And then for the first time I knew that fear does not protect us, and there is nowhere to hide from sorrow.

In early spring of last year she went to visit her sister in Rome. You've heard about that now. She was coming back by ship . . .

After her death my grief and remorse were almost insupportable. Some men, I believe, love more consciously than I and continually prepare themselves for a loss that they know will devastate their lives. But Rachel was so unobtrusive I had never understood the depth of my attachment to her.

There is something distasteful to me in talking about

this now, as though I were talking about an illusion, or an illness from which I later recovered – for I have recovered. You see me now an altered man. When I think of Rachel, I feel not sorrow but the memory of sorrow. And when I want to be happy, I think of another woman. All these events look strange to me now, exaggerated and mysterious, like something dreamed in delirium.

But at the time my grief made me ill. That is how this doctor comes into the picture. His name is Parsons. A nasty name, don't you think? And without the slightest cause on earth I now find that I dislike him thoroughly. Perhaps I blame him for his bad advice, for handing me the gift of leisure with his medical blessing.

He knew I loved music, and he advised me to go to Salzburg for the music festival to sweeten my wounds with Mozart and Beethoven. Instead I sold the house in Surrey and all our furniture and came to London.

I was incapable of work and unfit for human society. I gave up my job. I didn't want to sweeten anything. I wanted to punish. But who? And how? God was out of reach. There was only myself.

I was living alone in a hotel in Putney, and I saw no one to remind me of Rachel. I had answered none of my friends' letters, and no one wrote to me.

I sold or gave away everything that Rachel had owned and everything we had owned together. This had really shocked my friends, and a few of them came to the auction and surreptitiously bought up little things they thought I might want back later. Apparently it is more normal for grief to show itself by acquisitiveness – a desire to hoard and savour the past and to treasure things as symbols of happiness. Well, I was not entirely without these instincts, as you will shortly see, but they were not so strong at that time as others that worked against them. I felt that I wanted to fling everything away. My grief was like a sickness, a feeling of nausea towards the world.

I've just told you that I sold everything. But that's not true . . . During the past twelve years or so, I had slowly built up a small collection of Japanese colour prints, and these, and some of my books, I kept.

I had bought the prints mainly from dealers in London and Paris. They were a mixed batch, for I had not concentrated on any particular period, and only a handful were rare prints by early artists, these being generally priced too high for me.

The point about these prints is that Rachel found them grotesque. Rachel had a pink, sugary notion of beauty, and we never liked the same pictures, or the same books, for that matter, or even the same music. For I prefer beauty always a little soured. When it comes to me as a spoonful of syrup, I spit it out. Real beauty to me always expresses something total by containing a hint of its opposite. You might say, I suppose, that in my choice of prints I had rather concentrated upon the violent and macabre. At any rate, this was Rachel's contention. She liked the long droopy ladies of the Utamaro period – I liked them best when I related their dreamy romanticism to the life they led. There's a nice touch of contrast in that thought. And among my bundle of treasures there were several ghosts and some decapitated bodies. The Japanese find beauty in strange places – they recognise its totality, and do not hint at the opposite, but state it.

I know. I am digressing again. To put it briefly, Rachel regarded these prints as exclusively mine. She talked about 'our' house and 'our' furniture, but of 'your Japanese prints'. And when I sold the house and furniture I kept the prints with me and took them to London.

I can barely remember that time now. It was summer. The long days irked me. I used to wait for the night when I could sleep. I slept like a child. Deep, black, dreamless sleep. A lot of it. I suppose I was exhausted. I slept whenever I could. When the days were warm and fine I'd sleep in a deck-chair in one of the London parks. I liked St James's Park best because you could get near the water. I used to spend hours just looking at it.

I don't need to explain to you, do I, the fascination of water? The constancy that fills the heart with peace and stillness and the continual, unrepetitive changeability that keeps the imagination in motion, manufacturing, fabricating. Trite words, but in this case they need to be said. Under the trees by the island in the middle of the lake the water looked black and, where the light struck it, it was burnished and steely like the heart of a black pearl. It was impossible to guess its depth. Unfathomable. Impossible to see into it. Anything might have been lying beneath. When the ducks with their bright enamelled feathers swam over these places, they drew ripples across them, folds in the water that curved about their speeding breasts and disappeared in diverging lines, then curved around once more in sinuous, undulating patterns, as though something were moving under the surface of the water, or had just sunk beneath it.

But I wasn't always sitting in the park staring at the water. Don't imagine that. Sometimes it rained, sometimes there was a concert on the bbc and I'd lie on my bed and listen to that. Sometimes I went for long walks.

One day I found myself outside the Victoria and Albert Museum and, on impulse, I went up to the Print Room. I knew they had a collection of Japanese prints, but I had never seen them because I had never had time. Now there was all the time in the world.

I went through the catalogue and chose a name at random. Some early artist – Harunobu, I think. I only had one of his prints myself because they are too expensive for me to buy.

The attendant brought me a large red box full of mounted prints, and I sat for the rest of the afternoon looking through them. Perhaps the unhappiness I had been through made me particularly responsive to their beauty. I remember that day going home feeling more hopeful, as though I had just entered into a new phase of existence.

You might say that from that moment I began to move away from Rachel, to strike out, to live again. In my own way, you are probably thinking. I am sure you are saying to yourself that from that moment I began to pursue my own destiny, that it was a new birth and that up till then I had been living in a kind of womb with Rachel, secure from what I might be, from what I might do.

You would be wrong, of course, if that's what you're

thinking. I was not moving away from Rachel but closer to her. I was translating her. I have only escaped her now.

After that I spent part of almost every day at the Museum, looking at the prints. I began to make a systematic study of them. I bought notebooks and started making lists of signatures, inspection stamps and publishers' seals. From ten till five I lived contentedly in a serene and beautiful world where rain slanted over iris gardens, and women, frail and slender as tall flowers, tottered about on high shoes or reclined in a watery swirl of draperies. A world of paper kites and curved bridges – fireworks hanging suspended, red and gold in black velvet skies – and now and again a ghost and a corpse or two.

You will notice that I had given up my leisure. From ten till five I was working at my new hobby like a businessman. I would have made it nine till five if the Print Room had been open then. You might think I was well on the way to being sensible. Don't be deceived. But I needn't warn you. You are on the lookout for deception.

At length, after I had been going to the Museum for about six weeks, I decided to live closer in so that I would not have to travel so far every day, and moved to a private hotel in South Kensington.

It was situated in a quiet side-street south of the Old Brompton Road, a tall, narrow building with a pillared portico and a newly painted black door that shone like patent leather. The railings around the area were also black, and the thick, shiny paint gave them a curiously soft appearance so that you felt that if you leaned on them they would bend over like licorice.

The owner, an ex-army officer named Sinclair, whom everyone referred to as the 'Major', lived with his wife in a suite of rooms on the ground floor.

This hotel had been recommended to me years ago by a friend who said that it was quiet and inexpensive. It was lethargy as much as anything that made me take the room they offered me because, really, I hated the place at first sight.

Quiet, my friend had told me, and indeed it was, quiet as a grave. An extraordinary dry hush brooded like a presence on the stairway and in the corridors, the silence of a place that is run on a system of repressions and prohibitions.

It was curious, considering what I learned later about our friend, that so-called Major Sinclair. Of course, what went on in his little part of the world nobody ever knew. You might have supposed that he had sucked all the life out of those passages for his own private use.

Although the daily woman who saw to my room – Mrs Pride her name was – assured me that the place was 'full', I rarely saw anyone about.

But people were there all right. Sometimes I heard a soft sound behind a closed door; there were letters left on a polished mahogany table in the hall, and Mrs Pride had stories to tell of eccentricity and loneliness. The rooms, she told me, were mostly taken by visitors from various parts of the Commonwealth – Australians, Canadians, Indians. There were even a couple of Americans of the poorest kind. I don't know whether they talked to one another – they certainly never talked to me. And not that I wanted them to. Nothing would have irritated me more than little chats outside the bedroom door and over the breakfast table.

To avoid the slightest possibility of anything like this hap-
pening I took my breakfast in my room. Breakfast was the
only meal the Sinclairs served – you had your dinner out.
But you could always get tea and sandwiches.

My room wasn't too bad; large, bright and pleasantly
decorated. Even a watercolour on the wall was much better
than you normally expect to find in hotel bedrooms. It was
a landscape, probably of somewhere in Essex – an unsettled
sky lying low over sad, flat fields and autumnal hedges.

The room overlooked a small back garden and here too
the scene was autumnal, for it was September. Two large
elm trees dropped their yellowed leaves onto bare flower-
beds and sparrows hopped and scratched around a broken
urn on a cement pedestal in which, many months ago,
something had been planted.

I looked at the room on a Sunday afternoon and
told Mrs Sinclair that I would move in on the following
Monday. I didn't meet the Major then; he was away for the
weekend.

When I returned with my luggage on the Monday afternoon, the front door was opened by Mrs Pride, who led
me upstairs and unlocked my door. Almost the first thing I
noticed was the davenport.

'That wasn't there yesterday,' I remarked.

Mrs Pride was opening the window, for it was a fine,
mild day. She looked round enquiringly. 'What's that, sir?'

She was a middle-aged woman, almost lame with
the varicose veins that showed as thick ridges under her
stockings. Her hair was fading discreetly from blonde to
grey, and her face looked old by reason of its pinched and

harassed expression, a look you often see on the faces of people who have known a good deal of physical pain.

'That davenport – it wasn't here yesterday.'

It was standing opposite the bed directly beneath the watercolour. I was convinced that it had not been there before. I would certainly have noticed it.

The rest of the furniture in the room – the bed with green counterpane, the wardrobe, chest of drawers, writing table and chair, polished oak, dark, heavy and shining with a rather gluey finish – was all moderately new and looked to have been bought at the same time for just the purpose it now served, that of furnishing a bedsitting-room in a small private hotel. These things stood, as it were, in a no man's land of taste, probably pleasing no one and not drastically offending anyone either. But the little Victorian davenport, with its embossed red leather top and neat impractical drawers, had a look of individuality. It wasn't valuable, or even beautiful, but you felt that it had once belonged to someone in particular.

Mrs Pride stared at it. 'That's right, sir,' she said at last. 'Neither it was. If you don't like it I expect the Major will take it away and put it somewhere else.'

'No! No! I like it very much. Besides, I need a lot of writing space.'

'Well, it's a handy little thing.' She went to it and stood, stroking the leather with her fingers. 'It's just had its top re-done. The Major sent it off about a week ago, when the last gentleman was leaving. It used to be green, but I like it better now. That red makes a bit of colour in the room, don't you think, sir? You need a bit of colour in London, what with never getting the sun. It was an awful mess,' she added. 'I'm glad the Major finally got around to it. We had a little boy in here – regular little terror he was – cut strips off the top with his father's razor blades.'

I couldn't know that she was telling me things that were to be of the deepest interest and that shortly I would try to remember her every word. I was afraid she was going to be garrulous, and turned away from her to let her know that she had talked quite enough. She was a brave woman, probably loyal, certainly discreet. But depressing. I think it was her voice – it was colourless, flat and dreary.

'The old things are best, don't you think, sir?' she now said, and even in this remark she sounded defeated, as though the whole world was disintegrating around her. 'There's no wear in this new furniture.'

'Yes, yes.' I was really beginning to hate her. I hoisted my suitcase up on the bed and began unpacking.

She hovered about for a moment and then said mournfully, 'Is there anything else I can do for you, sir?'

'No, thank you.'

I gave her ten shillings, but she shook her head and said, 'No thank you, sir. It goes on your bill at the end of the week. It's a new rule the Major's made. Like they have in France. He thinks it's better for us.'

Obviously, in her view, it wasn't. A moment later she had gone and I was alone. I turned and looked at the davenport.

Now, I'll explain to you why I was so interested in it. It's probably not important but, then again, it might be to someone like you.

What had surprised, even startled, me was that at first

glance I thought it was my own. I had had one, you see, a walnut davenport that had been auctioned with the rest of our furniture. Of course, I quickly realised my mistake. This was not my davenport, it was just very like it. But that moment of recognition had shaken me. What had I felt? A rush of superstitious fear, not unmixed with joy and, then, disappointment . . .

You will have detected my inconsistency. Having divested myself of the past I now wanted it back and had been overjoyed when something of it had seemed to return to me. Even when I realised that I had been mistaken, I was glad to have the davenport. Though it had turned out to be a stranger, at least it resembled a friend. It was not until three nights later, however, that I looked inside it.

It was about seven o'clock in the evening. I had unpacked my clothes on the night of my arrival and had arranged my books in shelves alongside the bed. But I had not yet decided what to do about the prints. They were all mounted on thick white card of uniform size and were too large to fit into the drawer of the writing table, so I left them in their portfolios and laid them flat in the bottom of the wardrobe, which was just deep enough to take them. I decided to put the notebooks inside the davenport. Pencils and other odds and ends I put into one of the small side drawers. The notebooks themselves, along with some loose paper, went into the top.

This done I sat down in front of the davenport and looked at it, comparing it with my own. They were indeed very alike: the same width and height, the same number of drawers down the side, the same turned feet and round, wooden handles. My davenport had had a sliding panel that made a false bottom to one of the inside drawers, and I wondered if this one contained a similar hiding-place.

Taking out the notebooks that I had just placed inside, I dropped them on the floor and began to fumble about for the knob that would release the panel – if there was one. But there wasn't. Inside, the two davenports were constructed quite differently. This one had a little stack of drawers right at the back. I pulled them out and found a long, narrow space behind them. I couldn't see into it without bending right down and craning beneath the upraised lid. So I extended my hand and felt inside. Instantly my fingers encountered something within. It was soft and resilient. At first I thought it was alive – it seemed to stir under my touch, and my hand stiffened and drew back. But what could be living in there? I asked myself and, putting my hand in again, took hold of whatever it was and drew it out. It was a limp, sausage-shaped bundle about eighteen inches long, wrapped in pale green silk. Both ends were tied with old shoelaces.

I closed the lid of the davenport and sat holding my discovery in my hands. By now I was really curious. I was alone in that room, virtually alone in the world. I had nothing to do, nowhere to go . . . then I found this bundle of green silk. Or it found me. It was as though I had discovered a letter, addressed to myself, dropped by someone in the middle of a desert. It seemed significant and important, like a message. What could it be, I wondered, to have been put away so carefully and then perhaps forgotten? Was it something precious that had been treasured, something shameful that had been hidden, or merely something useless and forgotten?

Placing it across my knees I unknotted the laces and unfolded the silk. Then I sprang up, knocking over my chair – and it slithered away from me and dropped to the floor.

Lying at my feet, all spilled out on the carpet, was a long, thick hank of human hair.

CHAPTER 2

I stared down at it – with astonishment, with revulsion and, illogical as it sounds, with fear. I won't try, at this point, to explain that fear, except to say that it seemed to emerge from a sense of recognition. And it was gone in a moment.

After all, what was so extraordinary about a hank of hair? It had probably been left behind by some woman who had lived in the room before me. Fifty years ago, or less, you would have expected to find hair like this in almost any woman's bedroom. My mother had had her hair cut off when I was quite small and kept it as a thick plait that she some-times wore twisted around her head. I remembered that plait now, in the drawer of her dressing table, wrapped in a piece of white crêpe de Chine. But that was a long time ago.

Did women, these days, keep their hair after they'd had it cut off? I didn't know. I didn't know much about women these days. Rachel hadn't been what I would call a modern woman.

I picked it up and let it flow down over my hand. It was tied at one end with a thin strip torn from the green silk. I had thought at first that it was black, black as a crow's wing, but as the light fell upon it, the shining strands glittered with red lights. I began to fondle it idly, watching it shimmer in the light and enjoying the lissom, fluid way it ran through my fingers.

Yet I still felt a little wary of it. There was the strangeness of having found it – for even if it had belonged to a woman who had lived in the room, this did not explain why it had been hidden in the back of the davenport. And you'll probably think this absurd, but I had a curious feeling as I touched it of subjecting a living creature to intimacies which it, or she, was powerless to repulse and had not solicited. Had the hair been old and dry I might not have felt this, but it was fresh, shining and alive. A faint oiliness came from it onto my fingers. It seemed to me – and I recollect this impression in the days that followed as explaining something seemingly grotesque – that it still contained life from the body to which it had once been joined.

Is hair a living substance? I don't know, but at least it seems able to register degrees of physical well-being as it blooms with health or grows lank and dull with sickness. And once cut away from the body, wouldn't it slowly lose its sheen and then – as it were – die?

It seemed to me that it would, and that this shining lock that I held in my hand had not died yet, that there was still a measure of life waiting to ebb out of it.

How had it got there? Who did it belong to? And who had wrapped it in its green sheath and put it so secretly away? Probably I would never know. It was just one of those small interesting mysteries we are constantly encountering in our daily lives that probably have some perfectly simple explanation but, because of a collection of circumstances, seem inexplicable and strange. That's what I told myself. And I wrapped it up again and put it back.

Or rather I began to put it back. I had got as far as opening the lid of the davenport when I stopped and said to myself, Why should I hide it in there? After all, it's not my secret.

But when I came to put it away in the chest of drawers, I stuffed it right at the back of the bottom drawer underneath a pile of underwear. So you see, I was merely changing its hiding place from one that someone else had chosen to one of my own.

Don't ask me why I did this. I can't honestly tell you. Perhaps I did not like the idea of somebody finding it in my possession, which might happen if I left it lying around. What would I say? How would I explain such a thing? I would have looked a bit silly, wouldn't I, if Mrs Pride had found a handful of woman's hair lying on my dressing table. Silly and ashamed. And for some reason guilty. Right from the beginning I felt that. That some guilt attached to it, and that merely by finding it some of that guilt had rubbed off on me.

CHAPTER 3

Next morning I left the hotel at about nine-thirty and walked to the Museum. I was usually one of the first to arrive in the Print Room and always took the same seat at the third table, facing the clock.

I enjoyed those days in the Museum. It was warm and quiet – not the oppressive, anxious silence of the hotel, but a quiet that you find in places where people are reading or working contentedly. I liked the big, red print boxes stacked about, the dark, leather-topped tables, the blank face of the clock on the wall. There was a drab, comforting ugliness about the place, a kind of deliberate underestimation of all the treasure that was hidden away in the shelves in the back room. It reminded me of one of those shabby city offices with broken stairways, grimy walls and dusty, outmoded filing cabinets that are the ante-room to enormous wealth and power.

I still got a pleasant thrill when the attendant, pushing his trolley up to my table, dumped down a box in front of me – thirty or more valuable and beautiful prints – all ostensibly mine for as long as I liked to sit looking at them.

It seemed extraordinary that they should trust me with

these precious things – or anyone for that matter. What did they know about me and my character? No one was required to vouch for me. All they asked was that I sign my name in a book.

There were a few regular visitors like myself, who came nearly every day. One of these, a young woman of Levantine appearance, with black hair that hung lankly to her shoulders, a magnificent hawk-like nose and dark eyes, always arrived early and sat at the table in front of me. She invariably wore a grey skirt, a black sweater and woollen stockings of some vivid colour – bottle green, yellow or scarlet – and round her neck hung a chain made from discs of roughly beaten metal. A commercial artist of some kind, I supposed. She was making copies of nineteenth century costume prints.

I never spoke to her, but I liked her in a quiet way. Not knowing her name I referred to her in my mind as 'my Hittite girl' – I have no idea why – unless I imagined that Hittite women might have looked like her. Sometimes we glanced at one another, and though we never smiled I felt I knew her, and was conscious of her knowing me. She was part of the place, like the clock and the red boxes. I would have missed her if she hadn't been there.

I also liked one of the attendants, a bony young man with a brow so wide and prominent it looked as if it were packed and bulging with thought. He always smiled and said good morning.

You could say, I suppose, that nearly everyone who came to the Print Room did so because they loved the things that were kept there. And this made a bond between us all, like a silent and passive friendship. Looking back on those days now, I see that I was happy, without knowing it, of course. It was rather like my love for Rachel, that I hadn't known about either, and that I could only express after she had gone.

I am making it sound as though I was constantly looking about me at people in the room. I wasn't, you know. I was really absorbed in what I was doing. The room was there, all around me, like a cocoon wrapping me up. I sensed it. That was how it was. It wasn't until I found the hank of hair that day that I began to keep an eye on the people who sat at the back of the room and watched who came in and out of the door.

I arrived as usual just after ten. At ten-thirty my Hittite girl came in, wearing green stockings. She sat in her usual place, opened her sketchbook and a box of watercolours. She did terrible, insipid little drawings – Rachel would have liked them. I thought to myself that if there was any passion in her, then she spent it in her life.

I worked through the morning undisturbed and in my usual way. At one I had my lunch downstairs in the res-taurant and, after a brief stroll down Cromwell Road, I returned to the Museum and went back to the Print Room.

At three-thirty – I remember the time, for I glanced up at the clock above the black marble mantelpiece – I began to feel restless. Something tugged at my mind – a dim, nagging thought that wouldn't show itself. It was the kind of feeling you have when you have forgotten something, and you know this but not what you have forgotten.

I had been through a whole box of prints that day and now had the last of them in front of me. It was signed

'Toyokuni' and had been attributed to the second of the three artists who had used that name.

It was a theatrical print, showing one of the kabuki actors dressed as a woman. He stood in the foreground of the picture – a tall, wild figure wrapped in voluminous robes that were decorated in patterns of blue, purple and orange and that floated out from his shoulders and fell in stiff, angular folds hiding his feet. He held a staff tipped with a banner, and his long black hair streamed out around him and seemed to hang suspended about his head as though motionless in an element as thick as water. Magic, I thought to myself, magic, filling the air around him and lifting out his hair like waterweed – for behind the figure clustered a great crowd of foxes, which are known in Japanese mythology for their magical and malignant powers. You have to beware of a beautiful woman in Japan – she might easily turn out to be a fox. This woman, with her splendid robes and floating hair, would certainly be a fox.

It was the sort of print I liked. My kind of beauty, with a touch of something strange – that tall, majestic figure and those little yapping, sly fox faces crowding behind. I sat looking at it for a long time, enjoying its beauty, and then I wasn't thinking about it any more, or seeing it either.

For there came to me abruptly and vividly, like a visitation, a recollection of my discovery in the davenport.

I hadn't given it a thought all day. Now it came, or rather rushed, plunged, back at me.

The hiding place in the davenport, my hand touching something soft that was alive – the green silk bundle – my terror when I opened it . . . How vividly I remembered it and how extraordinary the whole thing now appeared.

Suddenly I wanted to hurry home and look at it again. Why? Don't ask me to tell you. Perhaps I felt that by examining it I might understand something about it.

Then again, this was, in a sense, our first encounter. He was sitting there directly behind me, though I didn't know it at that moment. I suspect that I sensed him – his hunger and his dread. You think that's far-fetched? Remember, I was living alone. The world might have been empty. You'd know it, wouldn't you, if somebody suddenly crept into your empty world and crouched in a corner of it, looking at you, wanting something you had, hating you, afraid of you. Well, we won't go into that – it's only speculation.

I began to pack the prints away. The catalogue was open in front of me. I closed it, rose to my feet and turned, for the shelves in which the catalogues were kept were behind me. Half a dozen people sat working at the tables at the back of the room. I remember a girl wearing black-rimmed spectacles shaped like butterfly's wings. I remember – you can trust my memory, don't forget there was very little going on that I wanted to recall – I caught a glimpse, so brief that all it brought me was an impression, of a man's face, pallid and white-eyed. He quickly bent his head. If I had been less preoccupied I might have stopped and waited for him to look up again, for that haggard stare seemed as personal and arresting as a hand laid on my shoulder.

CHAPTER 4

No one was about in the hotel when I opened the front door. The usual watchful quiet seemed to move forward to meet me as, with a deliberately soft footstep, I made my way up the stairs. Yes, I'll admit it, I was creeping in. Why? I don't know. Unless I felt I had become involved in something shameful, that I had secrets now.

I opened my door and locked it behind me. I went straight to the chest of drawers. In my anxiety I pulled at the drawer hastily and it stuck, so that I crouched on the floor for a moment or two, tugging at it, confused by a queer distress. It opened with a jerk.

The green silk bundle was still there, just as I had put it away. No one had made off with it. Who would? I took it out, laid it on the floor and untied the laces. A little late sun came through the window and shone in a pale bolt across the floor, and I laid the hair down directly into this beam of sunlight. It was thick and glossy as a blackbird's wing. It seemed strange to me now that at first sight of it I had recoiled and felt afraid.

I lifted it gently in my hand. I no longer felt that I ought not to touch it. It was mine. Like a man who digs up gold in his back yard I owned it by the right of discovery. I looked at it for a long time, then I folded it up carefully in the green silk and put it away.

There was a knock on the door, and Mrs Pride came in carrying a tray of tea and tomato sandwiches.

'I didn't know you were home, sir. I was quite surprised when I heard your voice.'

I had ordered tea. I didn't want it. I only wanted to talk to Mrs. Pride. I had to be careful. I had to work around to what I wanted. I asked her how long she had been working in the hotel.

Ten years, she told me – that was before Major Sinclair bought the house – the previous owner had recommended her and he had kept her on.

I had to listen to a lot of other unsolicited information. Her husband was dead; her daughter worked in Woolworth's in Oxford Street, which was hard on her legs; she had a younger sister living in Reading, who had married at seventeen and lost her husband and was about to marry again. Her low, sad voice made all this sound like an avalanche of disaster. When it was over I asked her, 'Was there a woman living in this room before I came?'

'Oh no, sir. What gave you that idea, sir?'

I said I had found some hairpins.

She shook her head. 'I can't think where they could have come from. Peggy doesn't use hairpins. Unless it was that Indian girl ... There hasn't been a lady in here for a long time. I can't remember when we had the last, about four years ago, before it was decorated. Because of the walls, you see, being green. We've got a lot of pink rooms, and the Major thinks it isn't right to put a gentleman in a pink room.'

'Who had this room before me?' I asked her.

'That was Mr Doyle.'

'Was he married?'

'Oh, no. That is, I don't know, but he lived alone like you.'

'What was he like?'

But either she didn't want to talk about him or he had baffled her and she didn't quite know what to say. He was young – I got that much out of her – and handsome, but there was some doubt about this; it was a question of taste. She didn't know what he did. He always seemed to have a lot of money. All his clothes looked brand new.

I said, 'What sort of a man was he? What was he like?'

She took a long time to answer. 'Well, I don't know as I can exactly say,' she said slowly. 'I never got to know the gentleman very well. I was upstairs then. Mrs Sinclair got me shifted down because of my legs. So I only did him on Saturdays, which is Peggy's day off.' Sunday was *her* day off, she felt compelled to tell me.

I supposed Peggy to be the young woman I had seen several times sweeping the stairs – a sturdy, pink-cheeked creature with the fresh, ready look of a country girl.

Mrs Pride was droning on. 'As it turned out I don't know I did myself much good by the change. It saves my legs a bit, but my arms are well nigh falling off by the time I've done number eight. That's the Indian lady across the landing. I've got to dread that room. Eight blankets she's got on her bed, sir. Think of that. And it's only September. Of course, she can't help it, poor thing. She comes from a hot country, a doctor she is too, very educated. I said to her, "If you've got eight blankets on your bed in summer, what are you going to do when the winter comes?" She said, "I suppose I shall just die," and that's the truth. It's a wonder she don't faint right away. I dread that bed, sir. It hangs over me all day.'

I said, 'This Mr Doyle . . . how long was he here?'

About two months, that was all. Where had he come from? Where had he gone? She didn't know.

I made no attempt to excuse my questions. For women like Mrs Pride, the telling of miscellaneous facts about the lives of others, the recounting of events, doesn't need any justification. To talk was to be alive – it didn't matter what you talked about. Talk wasn't conversation either, it was like your heartbeat – continual, monotonous, pointless. When it stopped, you stopped too. It was the expression of your consciousness.

'And who was here before Mr Doyle?'

'That was the professor, sir, and the little boy like I told you that cut up the davenport with a razor blade. They had the room for six months and then went to Canada. Not a day too soon either. It's no life for a little boy cooped up in London if you ask me, what with the Major being strict about noise and that kind of thing.'

I liked the sound of this little boy. He must have brightened the place up a bit. But those two didn't have anything to do with me – they didn't smell right. I let them go. 'You were going to tell me about Mr Doyle.'

'Was I, sir?'

You were, I thought, but you don't know what to say. What was odd about Mr Doyle? Unlike the professor and his son, Mr Doyle smelt exactly right.

Mrs Pride shied right off him, but she had a powerful subconscious mind, and I felt I detected its workings in her next remark. She said, 'London is a lonely place. That's what I keep telling Peggy. "What do you want to come to London for?" I say to her. "It's a lonely place".'

I said, 'Did he have any women friends?'

'I expect he did, but they never came here. Don't you think that's rather strange, sir? A young man, so handsome, if you like that sort of face, but he didn't seem to have any friends. No one ever rang for him.'

'Perhaps he was a stranger. I don't have any friends in London. You'll find that no one ever rings me either.'

She said, 'London is a lonely place. No doubt about it. I keep telling Peggy, "Loneliness is a girl's worst enemy".' She turned those drab eyes towards me. 'It's loneliness that drives people to be rash, you know – young girls taking up with strangers, and all that.'

I said, 'It seems Mr Doyle and I have a lot in common. Loneliness, no visitors and no telephone calls.'

'And no photographs,' put in Mrs Pride.

'Didn't he have any photographs?'

'Not one anywhere.' She looked around her as though to make sure that I didn't have any either. 'You notice things like that if you have to dust every day.'

'I don't like photographs,' I said. 'I don't like dead faces staring at me all day long. Perhaps Mr Doyle had reasons for disliking them too.'

'Well, they don't have to be dead, do they, sir?' said Mrs Pride, making a point that hadn't occurred to me. 'I always keep a picture of my niece by my bed at night. Such a sweet face. Not that I think you can't overdo it. You ought to see number three downstairs – an Australian lady – I suppose she misses her friends, so far away from home. It quite gives you a turn when you go in there.'

I could see that if I didn't stop here she'd be off again. Suddenly I longed to get rid of her. I cut her short and she left.

Now listen to what happened then . . .

CHAPTER 5

I had finished my tea. Mrs Pride had returned for the tray and left again. Night was falling and the quiet in the hotel was emphasised by the sound of sparrows squabbling for a perch on the cement pedestal in the garden. Then even this stopped.

I suddenly felt very tired and lay down on my bed. It was almost night in my room, but through the window and beyond the black boughs and withering leaves of the elm tree I could see a sky still saturated with white light and stained, low down over the roofs and chimneys, with a murky rose. For all I could hear of London noise I might have been dead and buried. The vast, heartless quiet of the city hemmed me round. London is a lonely place . . .

Now I want to explain that every night for the past month or more, in this hotel and in my old room in Putney, I had done the same thing. Every evening about this time I lay down on my bed, closed my eyes, and thought of Rachel. Or rather, I conjured her into my mind, until a picture of her formed in the darkness behind my eyes with great clarity. It was peaceful and soothing. It might have been sent expressly to comfort me.

I saw her dressed in white and floating, like Ophelia, in deep green water. Her eyes were closed, her pale face smooth and quiet. She was asleep and smiling. Her night-dress floated around her, and her thick, dark brown hair, spread out like a net, held her up, so that she sank slowly, and without waking, the green water washing over her until her face was obliterated, until it was no more than a white shape trembling under the tide, like a smooth stone lying on the bed of a river.

Of course, it couldn't have happened like that. The collision of the two ships had taken place at night in fog and storm. But as I didn't know how Rachel had actually died, my imagination could dispense with any possible but unproven horrors. Not that I actually thought about it – on the contrary. I had deliberately avoided wondering what might have happened. The image of Rachel, quietly drowning in her sleep, and happy, came to me unbidden, and once having come kept returning. There was never any change. She never awoke. Always the smooth face, untouched by fear, the closed eyes, the white body out-stretched in the net of hair . . .

It was this pale, smiling face that had jumped up to haunt me when I found the hank of hair in the davenport.

I had seemed to be molested by something from my imagination. For one hideous moment, it had seemed that I had created that twist of hair out of my dream, and when it lay there, swirling at my feet, I had seen a face looking up whitely out of it, the face of a dead, drowned woman.

By now it was past eight and I went out to dinner. I had noticed an Indian restaurant called the Madras not far away, and I decided I'd try it.

Yes, I know what you're thinking. I was looking for the Indian girl who might have been in Doyle's room and dropped her hairpins. The girl with all the blankets, whose bed was a nightmare for Mrs Pride. I'd run into her a couple of times on the stairs. I could remember a pair of large, black eyes, a long plait hanging down her back and a strange, attractive, musty scent. I had never spoken to her, nor she to me. We were strangers on our own threshold, but we might easily be acquaintances outside.

The September night was fine and mild. By staring hard into that murky darkness which, in London, passes for a sky, I could even pick out the faint glimmer of muffled stars.

Outside the hotel the street was quiet – a few people on the pavements, a car or two, that's all. I liked these streets at night when the life drains out of them and is secreted away within the big lit-up houses. The brooding quiet seemed expressly there to accommodate my solitude. I was alone with the motionless and the inanimate – the big, square paving stones, the spiked railings keeping the privacy of the wintry gardens. The brassy light of the streetlamps gilded the twigs of the cropped elms. A man with a dog gave me a quick, nervous look as he passed me, as though this were my world and he was a trespasser.

The Madras was tucked away down a side street with a dim neon sign sticking out over the door. It was a small place with too many tables in it – smoke and steam and too much light. I stood by the door looking about me at the white and dark faces.

Life, as a rule, deals in the unexpected, and when you go out looking for someone, you rarely find them. But she was there. I spotted her at once, sitting at a table for four in the corner – Indian students by the look of them, who wolfed their food and talked excitedly in their own language.

Miss Sacksena – that was her name – sat like a bundle with big eyes and a sleek head sticking out of the top. I could just see a bit of dull gold silk sari showing under the sweaters and Shetland scarf. I sat down where I could keep an eye on her. She had only just started her meal, and we finished more or less together. When she got up, I grabbed my bill and got to the door just before her.

I opened it, smiled and said, 'Can I walk home with you? We're neighbours, you know.'

'Of course, if you like.'

Out again in the silent streets, she walked at my side, a soft, drifting ball of tweed and wool. Even so she managed to be graceful. She was rather beautiful in a heavy, placid way and reminded me of Rachel. But I wasn't interested in her as a woman. She didn't have anything to do with my treasure, if that's what you're thinking – she had all her hair; a big, beautiful plait dangling down her back past her buttocks, as thick as my wrist.

We chatted for a while, beginning with Indian food and getting on to London and how she liked it and how long she was going to stay. She answered all my questions submissively. She hadn't been with the Sinclairs long – only three weeks. The hotel had been recommended to her by a friend who had stayed there almost a year. Only now she had gone north to Birmingham, and Miss Sacksena had her room. A pity – they could have gone out together and been company for one another.

I said, 'Did you ever meet Mr Doyle, the man who had my room before me?'

Yes, she had met him once or twice. He had borrowed some matches once to light his gas fire. And they met going in and out. He was always in a great hurry. She added, 'I thought he was a very spiritual man.'

This was a new line on Doyle and upset the idea I was building up of him. I wondered if I should take it seriously, or if I had encountered some kind of racial crankiness.

Racial crankiness, I decided later, for it turned out that Mrs Sinclair was 'very spiritual' too. And then she got on to music and ballet and talked some extraordinary stuff about 'getting in touch with the infinite' and 'mystic themes'.

CHAPTER 6

Next morning as I set out for the Museum I opened the door of my room to find Peggy on her hands and knees, brushing the stairs.

She was a pretty, plump creature with a high colour that London had not yet drained off, and a youthful, untidy blowsiness about her that was rather appealing. Her dress, which was too tight for her, was strained across her breasts and held together with a large safety pin. Her dull, straw-coloured hair was none too clean and dabbled in little curls on her moist neck. As she drew back, the look she gave me from her big brown eyes was at once knowing and innocent.

'Good morning, sir,' she said, and sneezed.

'Not a cold, I hope.'

'Oh no, sir. It's just the dust that bothers me.' She sneezed again and looked pinker, warmer and damper than ever.

I wanted to question her about the davenport and Mr Doyle – my predecessor who was so handsome, so solitary and so spiritual – but something warned me to watch my step. There was something about Peggy, not sly exactly, though that is the word that first came to my mind – but soft, open and untrustworthy. I imagined she would gossip heedlessly about the things that I had said, and I did not want it to be known that I was interested in the late occupant of my room. Mrs Pride was garrulous, but she had a harder and more reticent disposition.

At that moment a door downstairs opened and Mrs Sinclair appeared in the hall below. She began to walk upstairs and, seeing me talking to Peggy, fixed us with a pained and earnest look, as though she had caught us rioting on the stairs. Peggy lowered her eyes and continued with her work, and I went on my way.

I was later than usual at the Museum. The pattern of my new life that I had kept to so rigidly over the past two months was already breaking up. Like a precocious boy in his last year at school, I had outgrown my situation.

On my way to the Print Room, I dawdled through the long galleries. Two rooms had recently been closed for redecoration and were now open to the public. I walked through these, pausing over a case of Indian bronzes to look at fat, light-footed Krishnas and little terracotta heads with features as dim and mute as antiquity. And I wondered if Miss Sacksena's friend, who had had her room before her, had also been Indian and had also worn a long, thick plait of hair.

In the Print Room my Hittite girl was already at work. Her stockings were red that day and she wore a new necklace that looked to be made from pieces of thin silver wire and smooth white pebbles. She crouched over her feeble little drawings, her hair flopping forward on her sallow cheeks.

Looking at the back of her head, I thought, If I loved a woman, would I ask her to give me a lock of her hair? No, decidedly not. That sort of thing belonged to a time when love was wrapped up in sentiment and sex was discreetly ignored. You did not any longer go round carrying little gold curls in the back of your watch.

And somehow I was convinced that the owner of my hank of hair, if he was a man, was not a languishing youth prone to outmoded sentimentalities.

What kind of man was he, then, to have done something so eccentric and so uncontemporary? Not an ordinary man. Certainly not an ordinary man.

The time passed slowly. I couldn't concentrate on my work any longer. I kept looking at the clock. At twelve-thirty I got up and returned the catalogue to its place on the bookshelf. I had made up my mind to go back to the hotel for tea and sandwiches instead of taking my usual lunch in the Museum restaurant.

There were few people about, but just outside the hotel stood a black Austin, almost brand new. I paused at the top of the three steps that led to the front door and felt in my pocket for my keys. On the window to my right – one of the three ground floor rooms occupied by the Sinclairs – a curtain was jerked aside. I caught a glimpse of the Major's face – pale and ugly with anger. He was talking to someone in the room and, though he looked out of the window straight at me, I don't think he saw me. His eyes looked glassy, and I saw his lips moving in a tight, constricted way. Then he tugged the curtain over the window.

Poor wretch, I thought, imagining that he was giving his wife a taste of his temper. Actually, I had never heard him abusing her, but I assumed that he gave her a bad time. The contrast between them was so striking – the Major complacent, arrogant, ingratiating yet condescending; the woman nervous and over-eager – as to suggest to an almost sinister degree that he nourished himself upon his wife's nerves and sensibilities.

I was wrong, however. As I closed the front door behind me and paused in the quiet of the hall, I heard the sound of another voice – a man's voice – speaking low and indistinctly from the Sinclairs' room.

There was a moment's silence, then the Major boomed out, 'How dare you, sir! How dare you use that tone with me!'

There was something shocking about his loud, angry voice ringing out in the respectable hush of that house, where everyone instinctively spoke in whispers and trod on tiptoe. I halted and listened.

Sinclair's visitor answered in a low hurried mutter. I couldn't hear what he said, and I was just about to move on when the Major's next words pulled me up. 'I tell you it was empty! There wasn't a damn thing in it! I don't know what you're insinuating, but I don't like your tone!"

I can't tell you what I felt! A kind of wild elation . . . My heart was thudding with excitement. A sound came from the room like a chair scraping on the floor, and I looked quickly around me for some way of covering my eavesdropping.

Near the foot of the stairs stood a mahogany table with

an oval mirror in a gilt frame hanging above it. Letters for the residents and their weekly bills were always left on this table alongside a brass cigarette box and the latest issue of *Events in Britain*. There was a letter on the table now. I picked it up and looked at it.

Miss Mary Thompson. It sounded like an Australian name – I don't know why. Perhaps it was for the Australian girl with all the photographs. Living sadly, according to Mrs Pride, in a room peopled by the absent and the dead.

I glanced up into the mirror, into the face reflected there, and I hardly knew it as my own. A high, studious forehead with the hair receding, a pair of intent, eager eyes. Not good-looking. Rather nondescript. And yet I am sure Miss Sacksena would have called it 'a spiritual face'. Except for the mouth, which looked hungry and unsatisfied. It had never struck me before, but that mouth might have belonged to another man. Behind the reflection of my face I could see the light-green wall – how the Sinclairs went for green – and the door with its porcelain handle painted with pink rosebuds. There was no sound from the room. Either the scene had played itself out or was surging on in soft, turbulent whispers.

Then the handle turned and the door opened. A man came out – his back towards me – so that my first glimpse was of the back of a dark-grey suit. It looked brand new. And my last glimpse too, for it was then that Mrs Sinclair called me.

'Oh, Mr. Hand, I've been wanting to speak to you.'

She came towards me from the passage that led to the back of the house. 'Mr Hand . . .' I had to turn round. I could have murdered her.

'Yes, what do you want?'

She looked up in alarm at the sharpness of my tone. She was dressed to go out in a costume that was a good two inches too long in the skirt. Brown, with a heather fleck – you know those drab, frightened colours. The high-necked violet blouse made her face look as white as a kabuki actor painted with rice paste. She pulled at her cream cotton gloves and cast a nervous, puckered glance at the letters on the table.

It was about the bathroom. The one on my floor. The plumbers would be working there. Would I use the one on the next floor? Something utterly unimportant, maddeningly trivial.

The front door closed with a snap. He had gone. Mrs Sinclair dabbed at her brown hair and pushed a ragged lock under her awful hat. Well, I had lost him, and I really couldn't hate her any more, she was too pathetic. I felt ashamed for having snapped at her and said, 'You look very tired, Mrs Sinclair.'

It was fatal to say anything like that. Immediately she was wallowing in self-pity. 'I am,' she said in an exhausted voice. 'I wasn't well last year. There's so much to do. Derek and I were going to Portugal this winter. It's so cheap and the weather's beautiful. But the cook left . . .'

At that moment Sinclair opened his door and stuck out his head. 'May!' he boomed in his officers' mess voice. 'I want to speak to you.'

She started nervously and looked around with narrowed eyes. 'Yes, Derek, of course.' She glanced at me quickly, murmured something and hurried to him. The door closed behind them. I was alone.

Again silence, and again the unwritten laws of the hotel began to make themselves felt. No voice raised, no whistling, no singing, no music, no running up stairs, no visitors, no loitering in corridors. If you wanted any pleasure in that place it had to be private, secret, hidden away. On the other hand, I thought, as I went into my room, if you were secretive, if you had something to hide, this would be your kind of hotel.

I left my room at three-thirty. Time for an hour in the Museum.

When I got to the bottom of the stairs the door to Sinclair's room was open; Sinclair was standing near a table smoking a cigarette and looking at the back of his right hand. He glanced up as I went through the hall, then, coming quickly to the door, put out his head and said softly, 'I say, Hand, could I have a word with you for a moment?'

'Of course.' I went in, and he closed the door.

'Sit down.'

I had been in the room only once before, when I first came to look for a room and had talked to Mrs Sinclair. It was a pleasant room, in a typical South Kensington way. Big, with a high ceiling and tall graceful windows that allowed a good length of curtain on either side. The walls were panelled in light wood, and water colours hung about. The Sinclairs had rather good, if somewhat timid, taste in pictures – most of them were discreet and competent and melancholy, like the one in my room. There was some pleasant furniture. A rosewood table with a clawed brass foot caught my eye. In Victorian bookcases rows of leatherbound classics looked as if they had stuck together from long neglect. It was all dignified and discreet and dreadfully respectable.

Sinclair, on the other hand, looked overdone, as though he had dressed up to play the part of a retired army officer running a private hotel in South Kensington.

He had once been rather good-looking, I should imagine; now his face had shrivelled and sallowed and seemed to hang back behind a grizzled moustache that turned upwards so aggressively it looked stuck on. His eyes were a hard, light blue, flat and shallow and innocent of either humour or imagination. In dress he favoured a youthful jauntiness – daring tweed sports coats, shoes of gorgeously bright suede and silk scarves instead of ties. But he moved about in an abrupt, jerky way, as though he still felt he was wearing a tight-fitting uniform. You weren't allowed to forget that he had once been a soldier. He had a way of suddenly snapping his fingers and saying 'Right!' in a high, ringing voice, in the manner of one who is accustomed to making swift, audacious decisions.

At first he didn't speak to me but paced the room with slow, stiff strides and touched his moustache with the knuckle of his forefinger. At length he swerved round on me and, jerking a packet of cigarettes out of his pocket, shoved it under my nose.

'Thanks.' I took one.

I noticed there was a badge of some sort on his cigarette lighter, and the same badge appeared on the top of a silver cigarette box and again on a small pin stuck into his lapel. He obviously liked to go round well labelled.

'To get to the point . . .' he began gruffly. 'Something a bit awkward.'

I waited while he took another turn about the room.

'Chap who used to be here. Had your room, as a matter of a fact. Afraid I lost my temper with him.' He paused and gave me a rueful, conspiratorial smile.

I didn't say anything. I just sat, waiting. But I felt a thrilling, brimming sense of expectation.

Sinclair touched his moustache. 'Well . . . had your room, as I said. Claims he left something behind.'

'I see . . .'

'You know, Hand, I'm a patient sort of fellow. Try to do my best for everyone here. We get all sorts, you know. I try to pick 'em, sort the sheep out from the goats, you know what I mean. Even so we get all sorts. If a chap comes up to me and says what he wants like a gentleman, I'll go out of my way to help him. Not that I'm taken in, you know. I'd like to see anyone put something over *me*. But it's all in the way you go about a thing, eh? Not what you do but the way that you do it. This chap Doyle, that's his name. Freddy Doyle. I said to him, "Now, you damn well get out of my house and don't come back until you've learned to behave like a gentleman".'

'I don't understand. You say he left something?'

'So he says.'

'In my room?'

He had come to a halt by the rosewood table with the brass foot. Tapping his fingers on the polished top he glared up at a picture of Cheyne Walk under snow. 'Bit awkward,' he said gloomily.

'What did he leave?'

'He didn't get around to that.'

'I should have thought that would be the first thing he'd tell you.'

'He got as far as saying it wasn't my business.'

'It sounds quite a row.'

'Row!' expostulated the Major. 'Ill-tempered little twerp!'

'But what are you worried about?'

'Hand, I'll tell you frankly what happened. Always believe in putting my cards on the table. Right! You know in your room there's a davenport.' He paused. 'You haven't found anything, eh?'

'I know the davenport.'

'Quite. Well, it needed repairing. Leather stripped off the top. I've got a chap that comes around occasionally. Did some other stuff for me. Good worker too, put a whole new door on that cabinet. You wouldn't know to look at it, eh? Does everything himself. Makes a business by buying up all this big Victorian furniture and cutting it down for small Chelsea houses. Well, he was round here a couple of weeks ago with his van to pick up some chairs I was having repaired, and I thought while he's here he might as well have the davenport. Doyle was leaving that day. It was a bit sudden. He'd only told me in the morning. I went up to his room and found he'd gone out leaving his kit packed up. I had a look in the davenport – opened the top and a couple of drawers – it seemed to be empty, so I told my chap to take it away. I suppose I should have waited till Doyle came back, but damn it all, man . . .' He broke off.

I said, 'But when he came back he must have realised that he'd lost this thing. Why didn't he say something then?'

'Says he couldn't wait. Had an appointment. I wasn't there. My wife saw him leave, haring off down the stairs with two suitcases, didn't even say goodbye.'

'Why didn't he write, if it was so important?'

'That's it!' cried Sinclair, snapping his fingers. 'Could have easily dropped a line. It wasn't until *you* turned up . . .' He stopped and took another turn about the room. 'You don't know Doyle, by any chance?'

I got an inkling of what he was up to. 'Never heard of him.' He was staring at me distrustfully. 'What does he do?'

'Damned if I know. Seems to have plenty of cash. Brand new car. Said something about having come into some money. You didn't find anything, eh?'

'You asked me that before,' I said. 'The drawers of the davenport were all empty. You can come up and look if you like.'

'Damn it, man, I don't want to pry in your things,' he boomed, all the upright gentleman.

I sat quietly. I was really enjoying myself. It was years since I'd told such barefaced lies. But I'd gone too far inviting him to look into the davenport. He had begun to suspect me and kept shooting sharp, sly glances in my direction.

'Do you know what the blighter wanted me to do? I said to him, "I'll have a word with Hand and ask him if he's come across anything." Nothing wrong with that, eh? Not good enough for our friend Doyle. Wanted me to give him the key to your room while you were out, mind you, so that he could go up and fish around in your kit. Nearly threw a fit when I said I'd speak to you. "No, don't you say a word to *him*," he said. "I don't want *him* meddling in my affairs. I want to look for myself." Threatened me. Actually threatened me! Said if I didn't let him have the key he'd lay a charge against me.'

'He won't do that.'

'Why not?'

'Because people don't when they've got something to hide themselves.'

He narrowed his eyes at me. 'What's he got to hide?'

'I'm only going on what you're telling me.'

He was right in front of me now and stopped and looked down at me. 'Just what I've been thinking, sounded as if he knew you and wasn't letting on.'

I couldn't blame him for what he was thinking, but I pretended to be angry. 'In other words,' I said to him coldly, 'you think all this is just a pretext on Doyle's part for getting into my room. You're suggesting that we know one another, and that we have some kind of disreputable con-nection. You think I've got something that belongs to him and that he's trying to get hold of it.'

'Oh, I say . . .' he began.

I stood up and turned to the door. 'I've never seen nor heard of your friend Mr Fred Doyle.'

He began to stutter. 'Look here, he's not a friend of mine. We've knocked around a bit. Spent a night or two at the pub. But that doesn't make him a friend of mine.' It was as I suspected. He was frightened. Doyle had some hold over him.

I paused on my way to the door and looked back. 'Would you like to know what I think?'

Now he was falling all over himself to be pleasant. 'I'm at sea, old man, absolutely at sea. This chap Doyle, most extraordinary. After all, why should he be so dead set against *you*? Came and talked to me, all right, but, when I said I'd speak to you, he hit the roof. You must admit it's a bit odd.'

'I think there's a perfectly simple explanation. Possibly Doyle did leave, or thinks he left, something in the davenport. You might get hold of your furniture friend, he may have come across it. It's probably something very personal that Doyle doesn't want anyone to see. And the reason why he doesn't want to run up against me is because he's afraid I might have seen it and he's ashamed to face me. He hopes it's still there. That's why he wants to go and have a look. But if by any chance I had found this thing, well, he's not going to stand the risk of running into me. It's obviously something a bit odd, embarrassing. Perhaps something he ought not to have.'

He looked up suddenly, his eyes bright with an indecent glitter. 'I say, pornographic pictures, or something like that!'

'Something like that.'

'But, damn it! Why would the man come back? Why wouldn't he just write them off?'

'Perhaps he was attached to them. Couldn't replace them with anything else as good.'

Sinclair looked doubtful and knuckled his moustache. 'By Jove! Rather fits the book, doesn't it?'

'It fits the book very well.'

'Hadn't thought of that. Come to think of it, he looks as if he might be that sort of chap. Something about him, you know, not quite . . . all the difference between that sort of thing and a good smutty joke. Ha! Ha! Rather enjoy a smutty joke myself. It's got to be good, mind you. Can't stick filth for filth's sake. I say, have you heard the one about the cross-eyed gynaecologist?'

The anecdote was brief and disgusting. Sinclair roared with laughter and slapped me on the shoulder. 'I say, if you ever come across those, you know, postcards, photographs, what have you, wouldn't mind having a look at them.'

With his hand still on my shoulder he walked me to the door. We were the best of friends. 'I say, I hope you don't think I, er . . . well, the whole thing was a bit odd, you know. Enjoyed our little chat. How about dropping into the pub one evening and having a drink? Usually go to the Three Bells down by the river. Not too close to home, you know.' A dig in the ribs. 'Not too far away either. Don't usually have much to do with the people here, you know. Never mix business and pleasure, eh? Gets a bit awkward when you have to send in a bill at the end of the week. Ha! Ha! Still, make an exception every now and again when I meet someone of my own sort.'

I murmured something noncommittal, but he tried to pin me down. 'What about one night next week? Usually go away for the weekends. Got a little place down in Essex. Does you good to get away from the bright lights. What about Monday? Tuesday?'

But perhaps he wasn't trying to pin me down after all, because while I was thinking up an excuse, he hit me on the back and shouted 'Right!' as though it were all arranged.

CHAPTER 7

That night it began to rain, and a light drizzle continued throughout the following morning. It must have kept people at home, for the Print Room was almost empty. I filled out a card for two boxes of prints, and when they arrived, looked through them as you might look through a magazine in a waiting room.

I was convinced that Doyle knew me and was watching me. The man who had been sitting behind me two days ago, I was sure he was Doyle. The incident had seemed unremarkable at the time. In retrospect it seized my imagination. It became the point upon which other incidents met and diverged. I thought that over the past few days I had heard footsteps following me, that a slight figure in a dark suit had stood looking after me on a street corner. I began to feel that someone out of my sight was yet present, even recognisable. At any rate, I was sufficiently familiar with him to eliminate and dismiss, and, looking around me in the street or at people strolling through the Museum galleries, I could say with perfect certainty, 'It's not he . . . not he . . .'

I believed that he wanted to speak to me but didn't know how to approach me. He had been following me. He knew my habits, and I continued in my old way so that he could plan our encounter.

In the meantime my old pleasures were spoiled. I was inhabiting a world that had died around me. Everything had changed: there was a forlornness about the room; the atmosphere you sense in a place you are going to leave, with no hope of return. The Museum had been a refuge for me. How much more beautiful than the world outside were those Japanese gardens with their bowed bridges and slender willows. I had been happy in that faded, silent dominion. But my attachment to it had been a negation, and it could not hold me against the pull of my new obsession.

I sat, bored and impatient, one eye on the door. But people came and went, and Doyle was not among them. Keeping carefully to my old routine, I waited till one, then put the prints away and got up to leave.

Closing the Print Room door, I began to stroll through the Print Room Galleries to the staircase at the end.

These rooms were being used at that time for an exhibition of American lithographs, and I glanced at some of these as I went by. I passed a man wearing a dark suit, standing with his hands behind his back before a picture of an owl. I felt annoyed with him for standing so close to the picture, right in the way of anyone else who might want to look at it, for it was a very striking piece of work, the owl staring out with round yellow eyes through a branch of red maple leaves; an unusual, broken composition. It might have been Japanese.

I moved across to the windows on the other side of the gallery to see if it was still raining. And it was. I could look down onto a quadrangle, green lawns intersected by straight white paths, some empty wooden seats with litter baskets beside them. The red brick and yellowish, grimed stone of the Museum shone with quiet luminosity. A Buddha, black and shining with the rain, set an example of contentment and contemplation. A happy thought on the part of the Museum authorities and, if you were sitting out there eating sandwiches, good for the digestion.

'Excuse me, did you drop these?' It was a high, thin voice, with a slight tremor.

I turned. He held a pair of yellow skin gloves in his hand, which was stretched out to me like an appeal. The eyes of the owl in the lithograph were twin yellow circles behind his head. 'Did you drop these?' he said again.

I shook my head.

His hand fell to his side. For a moment he looked disconcerted, then he gave me a big, empty smile. 'Must belong to someone else.' He stuffed them in his pocket.

He was younger than me. About thirty, I should say. Not tall, and rather slight. His face was long, narrow and pale. The eyes, set in deep, scooped-out sockets, gave an impression of darkness and lustre, but later, when I looked more closely into them, I noticed that the iris was clouded by milky patches that seemed to film his gaze and in certain attitudes made him look white-eyed and blind.

He was handsome, all right. The hair grew on his beautiful head in thick, waving tongues. His nervous, sensitive, mongrel face, without sentiment or gentleness, repelled and attracted me. It was a face without sentiment or gentleness. I waited for him to speak again, wondering what he would say.

And looking into my face for meanings behind my eloquent, sympathetic eyes and worldly mouth, he must have been wondering to what degree he could trust in my obtuseness or my understanding and whether he would have to fear me most in what I could grasp or in what was beyond me.

There was a moment when I thought that he almost decided to confide in me. If so, he didn't trust his instinct, and the chance was lost. Instead, he began to sidle around me like a cautious dog.

He jerked his head at the Print Room door. 'You come here a lot.'

I raised my eyebrows.

'I've seen you in there,' he said.

I didn't help him. If this was his game, I was going to let him take the strain of it. I waited, watching him. I noticed the careful attention he paid to his dress. He wore a well-tailored dark suit. Good cloth, nothing wrong with it. But somehow on him the effect was flashy.

'What do you think of all this?' he said in that high-pitched voice, thin as a woman's.

'I've hardly looked at them.'

'I don't like art. It's not real life.'

'No,' I said. 'It's an improvement on it.'

'Is it?' he asked me suspiciously.

Obviously he didn't have much education. I couldn't even begin to guess at his social background or the environment that had spewed him out. He was a bit of everything, put together out of the dust of a dozen cities. The heir to a multitude of thefts and assassinations.

We had begun to walk slowly down the gallery towards

the stairs. He pointed at pictures as we passed them. 'Look at that, that's not a bird,' he jeered. 'Call that a woman, that's not a woman. Now I like that.' He paused. 'I like pictures of boats. I'd say that was a good picture. I wouldn't mind having that picture.'

It was an ordinary, commonplace thing of fishing boats in the south of France. An ordinary picture for an ordinary man. I was disappointed in him. But he was only feeling around for something to say.

'That looks like real water,' he told me in a satisfied, confident tone, as though he was pleased with the show he was putting on. 'It's not easy to paint water.'

'These aren't paintings,' I told him.

Immediately there was a hint of temper. A pulse jumped in his cheek. It was a thinly covered face with several weak places in it where the nerves throbbed at the slightest hint of anger or frustration. 'Well, *drawings* then. I suppose they're *drawings*, are they? I haven't studied pictures like you. I've got better things to do with my time. Like I was saying, it isn't easy to draw water. Stands to reason – it's on the move all the time; it flows, you see.'

'Like hair,' I said. 'Like a woman's hair.'

He went as white as a stone, and his eyeballs turned upwards under their closing lids. I thought he was going to faint, but with a great effort he pulled himself together. Abruptly, and without another look at me, he hurried on ahead down the stairs and disappeared around the first landing.

I didn't hurry. I knew he'd wait for me. Talking to me hadn't been easy for him. In that little scene with the gloves he had been really wrought up. He wasn't going to run off now and give up the ground he'd won.

I descended the staircase slowly, between cupids and satyrs, rams' heads and dolphins. It was a queer setting for the beginning of our struggle. I think he felt at a disadvantage. It wasn't his world.

On the landing there was a stained-glass window, a Madonna and Child, the Child holding a spray of silver flowers and with two purple doves at his feet. Down another flight and I was in the Italian Renaissance.

And he was waiting for me, by a little shell-white della Robbia boy playing bagpipes.

I said, 'I thought you'd gone.'

'I'm like you,' he said sullenly. 'I'm on my way out.'

We walked out together, and now he jeered savagely at the white porcelain altar pieces and the exquisite Florentine marbles. When we got to the front door I said, 'Aren't you going to hand in those gloves?'

'Not on your life! I found them, didn't I? They're good gloves.'

They were too. Obviously his own. I said, 'That's the way I look at things. What you find you keep. After all, if someone is fool enough to lose them, that's his lookout.'

He didn't say a word but just shrivelled up inside his coat. I had the impression now that he wasn't very intelligent. Otherwise he would never have left me an opening like that. But I also felt that his instincts were as sharp as an animal's. He was as cunning as a cat in the dark and, although he might not think cleverly, he would act cleverly, without having to think at all.

Outside it was still raining, but not so heavily as to trouble us, and we walked side by side over to South Kensington tube station.

It was the kind of London day I like. Still, not too cold, dull, but with a tender shine behind the mistiness. Weather that particularly suits those dignified, aloof and secretive streets. Hardly any colour anywhere, the buildings all varying tones of grey, the iron railings jet-black, like strong pen strokes. Any leaves that remained on the trees had long since lost their green and withered to a spectral brown. And in that neutral scene the big, red buses whirling by.

He was talking again, suggesting that we have a bite to eat. I noticed the way women looked at him. We had just crossed Cromwell Road when we passed two young girls wearing tight ski pants and sloppy sweaters, who stared at him in an open, unselfconscious way, the way people stare at someone they consider to be public property, someone either very famous or very beautiful. And a little further on, a rather handsome, middle-aged woman, who should have known better, gave him a long, suggestive glance. He could have picked up all of them if he'd wanted to.

It annoyed me to see him creating all this attention. I suppose I was a bit jealous. I've never expected to attract a lot of women. Well, I'd be a fool. But we were rivals, in a way.

We had lunch in a snack bar. There were some high stools around the counter and a lot of little tables covered in red Formica. I remember the Formica because when Doyle put his hand on the table his fingers looked as white as wax candles. Here it was the same story over again. The waitress took an instant fancy to him. She was a plain thing with a sallow, pinched face that she had tried to brighten up a bit by pencilling smudgy black lines around her eyes. She hovered about our table, swishing her skirts and patting her hair. Doyle hardly spared her a glance.

Even so, it annoyed me. What did they see in his bastard beauty? Couldn't they smell him for what he was? I only had to look at him to know he was corrupt.

Notice the word. I mean it. I know you've got different ideas about Doyle. And you're wrong. There's nothing unusual about him – nothing that wasn't normal once. He's simply corrupt, and he corrupted everything he touched. I ought to know.

We had ordered sandwiches and tea. He hadn't said anything for a long time, but when the sandwiches came he started again, trying to make conversation. Suddenly he said, 'When I've finished I'm going back in there to give back those gloves.'

'That's very honest of you,' I said.'

'They don't belong to me,' he said. 'They prey on my mind, that's what they do. Having something that doesn't belong to me.'

He hadn't touched his sandwiches. He was sitting hunched up, his shoulders drawn forward, looking straight at me. It was then that I noticed the cloudy patches in his eyes. They were like a mist forming over the eye and preventing you from looking into them. Perhaps this was what Miss Sacksena had seen when she called him 'a spiritual man'.

I answered in a light, bantering tone. 'Good Lord, you have got a delicate conscience. I'm afraid I haven't got your scruples. If I had found those gloves I would have hung on to them.'

The little pulse started jumping. 'You shouldn't,' he said, and it was a whisper, but it sounded like a shout. 'You haven't got any right to do that. They belong to somebody else. You shouldn't keep what doesn't belong to you.'

I laughed. 'I'm a communist. I don't believe in private property.'

'You've got your debt to society.'

'I suppose I have. But as long as I'm all right, I don't care about society.'

He half rose to his feet. 'That's stealing!' he spat out at me.

And I leaned back to escape his hatred that was like poison spurting out of his mouth. 'There are worse crimes than theft.'

He had gone pale, and his face seemed to petrify around his eyes. 'What are you talking about?' he said faintly.

'I'm not talking about anything in particular. I'm just saying that if I find something that used to belong to somebody else, and I like it and want to keep it, then I can't see any reason for giving it up. And if the person who lost it wants it back, he can't expect to get it for nothing, because now it belongs to me.'

'Money . . .'

'I didn't say anything about money.'

I had just been talking at random, and it wasn't until later that I realised I had made him a proposition. There wouldn't have been any point in flatly refusing to hand over his lost treasure. I would have simply invited him to murder me. I had to state a condition, offer a glimmer of hope. He could have it at a price but, at the time, I hadn't the slightest expectation of his being able to pay it. It took him a while to take up the challenge. The risks involved were almost as great as doing nothing at all.

He looked at me out of the sides of his eyes. 'Is that your last word?'

'That's final.'

He sat saying nothing, white and rigid, fighting visibly his hatred of me and his rage in his defeat. Then he got up and began to move away.

He looked back and said, 'See you', in a mechanical way, as though he had forgotten who I was. And then he was gone.

That evening when I got back to the hotel I went to my room, locked the door and took out my hank of hair.

It is very difficult now to describe to you my feelings as I looked at it and held it in my hand. So much has happened to disperse my memories. It is always difficult to re-enter a condition of ignorance, and in those days my hank of hair was still an object that was complete in itself – a token, a symbol, something you keep for its own sake, like a flower or a letter. I never thought of it as part of something else and therefore incomplete, something torn away, hacked off, evidence of mutilation.

For me it was mysterious and beautiful. And it had the power of inducing in me an extraordinary rush of feeling, all the more so now that I knew that someone wanted to take it from me. It seemed to me that nothing on earth would persuade me to part with it.

I was wrong, of course. I would be only too ready to give it up the moment it disclosed its meaning. Then it would lose its power over my imagination, and my desires would reach beyond it.

CHAPTER 8

The next day was Sunday and the Print Room was closed. I stayed inside most of the day, expecting that Doyle would try to get in touch with me. But there was no sign of him. When I went out to dinner in the evening, nobody followed me. I looked into the shadow of every doorway, but nobody waited.

Tuesday passed, and the exhibition of American lithographs was being dismantled. People were wandering about, carrying pictures; other pictures were stacked up, their faces against the wall. The rooms were closed to the public and shut off by barriers, and to get to the Print Room, I had to take the staircase near the Exhibition Road entrance and go through Book Illustration, Decoration and Book Binding. I disliked this new route and resented having to take it. I missed the della Robbia Madonnas, the boy with the bagpipes, and the stained-glass window on the stairway, with its burning blue, its purple doves and silver flowers.

No sign from Doyle. Yet I knew he must be planning some new manoeuvre. It was unthinkable that having gone so far he would disappear and leave me holding the prize.

The waiting made me tense and watchful. Every time I went to take out my hank of hair, I expected to find it gone. I changed its hiding place a dozen times.

On Wednesday morning plumbers started work on the bathroom next door to my room. There were two of them, a small, foxy-looking man with bright, witty eyes, and a lanky youth with a pink face and a lot of tightly curled, wet red hair. They were a likeable pair, given to jokes and high-spirited whistling. That is, for an hour or two, for the hotel quickly worked its oppressive spell on them. Mrs Sinclair kept hovering on the landing outside my door, watching them with her puckered eyes, and then ordered Peggy to put newspapers on the stairs so that they would not soil the carpet with their boots. She also took away a picture, as it might be in danger of being blown down by their gusty breathing, and she always managed to be there when they were drinking their tea, which must have made them feel that they were drinking too much of it too often.

Soon the cheery cockney voices sank to whispers, the tuneful whistling stopped and the only sound the two men made was a dull, vindictive hammering.

I only saw Sinclair once that week. It was Friday. When I came back from the Museum, he was standing by the table in the hall putting out the envelopes that contained our weekly bills.

He looked up when he saw me, and an annoyed, alarmed expression showed in his face for a moment. Then he nodded, muttered something and made for his door with a long, stiff stride. I had the impression he wanted to keep out of my way, and supposed that he regretted having invited me to have a drink with him. But it was more than that. By that time he must have seen Doyle again and handed over the duplicate key. But I expect he laid down some conditions: 'Not while I'm here.' 'You wait till I'm out of the way.' ' I don't want to be mixed up in this.' Because next morning he was off for the weekend, dressed for the part in checky, leather-patched tweeds, the back of his car full of golf clubs and suitcases.

On Sunday morning I left my room at about ten and met Peggy on the stairs, looking moist and warm in her tight blue uniform. She stood back against the wall to let me pass. 'I was just going to do your room, sir. Will you be out for a bit?'

'Yes,' I said. 'For an hour or so.'

I always took a long walk on Sunday mornings.

Her face looked fresh and pink against the pale green wall. She was like a ripe plum, ready to drop into some-body's mouth. But that morning, instead of her usual melting glance, she kept her eyes lowered. I went on down-stairs, wondering what had made her suddenly shy.

Mrs Sinclair appeared in the hall below, wearing a brown coat and a green felt hat with a little peak in front, giving it that slightly military air beloved by Englishwomen. She was on her way to church, and I walked to the end of the road with her, until she turned left to an ugly grey Methodist church, and I went on into King's Road. At this point it began to rain, so I bought an assortment of Sunday papers and went into an epresso bar to read them.

You see the point? Sunday, the Major away for the weekend, Mrs Sinclair at church, Mrs Pride's day off. Only

Peggy holding the fort. If I had had any sense I would have realised what was going to happen.

The espresso bar was a dingy place decorated with murals depicting some hot, sunny land. Mexico, I imagine, to judge by the cactus plants and big yellow hats that were splashed about. But the clear colours had already been greyed by London grime, and the painted scenes looked indescribably sad and defeated.

I glanced through the headlines.

Further wage claims ... measures to stop inflation ... another girl found naked and dead in a Hampshire wood ...

There was a photograph of her. She had short, blonde, curly hair.

Outside on the pavement umbrellas went up. The rain was falling heavily, and it looked as though a walk would be out of the question so, rather than spend the morning in that depressing dream of a sunny land, I decided to make a dash for it back to the hotel.

I arrived, pretty well drenched, and paused in the hall to get my breath. There was no one about – no sound came from the rooms at the back. The place might have been deserted. For some reason I thought of Sinclair and wondered what he would do in the country on a wet weekend. Sit in a pub all day, probably. Or perhaps he had female company.

I went on upstairs, very quietly, not because I had any notion of what was going on in my room, but in deference to custom.

When I reached the landing outside my door I heard a

voice. And I stopped and listened. Then I heard it again. Very quietly I turned the handle and opened the door.

They did not hear me. They stood with their backs to me, bending over the davenport. They had raised the lid and all the papers that I kept within were neatly stacked on the floor. Doyle's hands were feeling about inside.

Peggy stood close beside him, peering over his shoulder. She must have felt a draught from the open door, for she glanced back. Her grey eyes widened. She let out a little shriek and clutched his arm.

He didn't turn or move at all. He became quite still, in that crouched attitude, like an animal freezing against danger.

Then slowly he straightened his back, withdrew his hands from inside the davenport, closed the lid and turned. His face was quite composed.

I pretended to be furiously angry. I did it so well I convinced myself, until I *was* furiously angry. 'What are you doing here?'

He really was rather dignified. In that high, squeaky voice of his, he said, 'You've got something that belongs to me. I came to get it.'

'Why didn't you ask me for it?'

'I did. You refused to give it to me.'

I couldn't deny this. Suddenly I felt he was getting the better of me. So calm, so composed. I became really angry. 'You broke into my room,' I raved at him. 'I could put the police on you!'

He didn't reply. He must have known that I faced and rejected that decision days ago.

Peggy let out a whimpering sob. Without taking his eyes from my face, Doyle put out a hand and touched her on the arm. 'Go outside. Go on, clear off! Leave us alone.'

She scuttled for the door, but I grabbed her arm and pulled her back. 'You stay here. I want you here!' I gave her a shove toward the bed, and she sat down on it, gasping. 'Now . . .'

'You've got something of mine,' said Doyle. He looked dull and meek standing there. 'I was only looking for that. I haven't got anything against you. I wasn't after anything else. Give it to me!'

'I did find something in the davenport,' I said. 'But I'm not handing it over to you. It's not yours. I'll only give it up to the person it belongs to, and that's not you.'

He made no movement. There was no alteration in the expression on his dull face. But he understood all right.

'Now, get out,' I said.

His hat was on the foot of my bed. He glanced at it and made two slow steps towards it. The movement brought him closer to me. For a fraction of a second he hesitated, then sprang at me. His hands clawed for my throat.

It all happened in an instant, but I knew he was desperate, and I was ready for him. I was heavier than he was, and I had an elementary training in jujitsu on my side. For a moment his face was close to mine. I looked right into his eyes and imagined that I saw the milky patches cloud over them, blotting them out in a hard, pearly shine. I forced him back, his body arched like a bow. In the next moment he was down on the floor.

'Now, get out,' I said, standing over him.

He got slowly to his feet and stood, swaying slightly.

'Don't forget your hat.'

He went to the bed, picked up his hat and put it on carefully, pulling the brim down over his eyes. Then he went slowly past me to the door, without a glance.

I turned to Peggy and jerked my head. 'You too.'

She was so terrified she didn't hear me. I said it again, and she got up and stumbled to the door.

CHAPTER 9

Now, it must be obvious to you that right from the beginning, from the moment I found the silk bundle in the davenport, Doyle and I were not alone in this affair. There had always been a third character, a woman, who had not yet played any part in our little drama and whose shadowy presence hovered beyond the range of speculation.

Who was she, this woman with black hair? And what was, or had been, her relationship with Doyle?

By now I was pretty certain that I knew, until Doyle himself, by his next move, shattered the whole fabric of my suspicions. You're going to say that I challenged him. I've already admitted that I did, but I never imagined that he'd take me up, that he *could* take me up, even if he wanted to.

Looking back now I see how rash his move was, and how clever. With an uncanny knowledge of my character he saw at what point I would cease to oppose him and understood where I would be weak and flexible. Well, you're going to say, we had a lot in common. We could both gauge the other's reactions because neither of us had any feeling that we were dealing with an unusual man.

It was Monday afternoon. Five-thirty. I had been home for about an hour, because I was leaving the Print Room earlier now.

I was sitting by the window reading, when there was a knock at the door. 'Come in,' I called, closing my book and putting it down on the floor. The knock came again, so I got up and opened the door. Mrs Sinclair stood in the threshold, looking at me with that tight, puckered glance I had come to learn meant that she was feeling tired or angry or martyred or that she had a headache.

'There's someone to see you downstairs, Mr Hand.'

'To see me? Are you sure?' Instantly I thought of Doyle.

'She says she has an appointment with you.'

'A woman?'

I was about to say that there was some mistake and that no one had an appointment with me, but Mrs Sinclair spoke first. 'Would you come downstairs please, Mr Hand? You know we don't allow visitors in the rooms.'

This enraged me. I had been in the place for over a fortnight and had she searched London she couldn't have found a tenant more ready to submit to her oppressive respectability. 'Please send her up here immediately,' I said.

She glared at me through screwed-up eyes, then closed the door and went downstairs. I waited, wondering whether I was wasting my sympathies on the wrong member of the Sinclair family. A moment later a light tap sounded on the door.

A young woman, hardly more than a girl, stood on the threshold. A plump, smiling girl with big, grey, black-lashed eyes and a skin like peaches and cream. She wore a grey coat, tan gloves and a yellow scarf tied around her head.

She smiled at me. 'Are you Mr Hand?'

I said I was.

'My name's Gladys Wilson. I'm Fred Doyle's girlfriend.'

I found myself holding her hand. Perhaps I said something – I don't remember what. The confusion in my thoughts made me dumb and stupid. The moment was not unlike that other moment weeks ago when I first found the hank of hair in the davenport. There was even a touch of horror in it. Freddy Doyle and this plump little dewy creature . . .

'You're just like Freddy said.' Her grey eyes looked at me, limpid and innocent and stupidly incautious. 'Aren't you going to ask me in?'

'Of course.' I pulled up the most comfortable chair for her, arranging it so that she was facing the davenport, but she did not once look at it, though I noticed her glance up at the picture above. When I turned from closing the door she was sitting down, one leg crossed over the other, pulling the glove off her right hand. She had small square hands and rather dirty nails. All the time she was looking around her in an interested wide-eyed way like an exploring puppy. Then she looked at me and smiled again. There was not the least hint of reserve in her manner. We might have been friends for years. I felt like saying to her, 'Go back home, little girl. You oughtn't to be let loose in this wicked world. Go back to your mother till you've grown up and learned to be wary.'

'Nice here,' she said.

'Do you think so?'

'Better than my place. You've got a bit of a view. I miss a good view. You know what I've come for, don't you?'

'I've got no idea.'

'Freddy said you'd talked about it.' She looked at me confidently and, when I said nothing, continued. 'You've got something for me. He said you'd promised him you'd give it to me.'

I was trying to think, and my mind was a whirl. I suspected a trick. Every nerve in my body cried out, telling me not to trust Doyle. And yet how could I suspect this girl? She couldn't have been more open, more ordinary. She was astonishing in her commonplaceness, the last thing on earth I had expected to turn up.

I said, 'Did he tell you how we happened to meet?'

'He told me that you'd talk and talk and that I wasn't to take any notice or answer any of your questions because you'd promised you'd give it to me. And there isn't anything else to say.'

'If it belongs to you.'

'He was right, wasn't he? You do go on. You can't fool my Freddy. He knows about people. There's nothing he doesn't know.'

'You admire him, do you?'

'Of course I admire him. What a funny thing to say. He's my boyfriend. There you go again, putting me off.' She was laughing at me, but serious at the same time.

'How do I know it belongs to you?' I insisted.

'Of course it belongs to me. Freddy said you'd only have to look at me and you'd know it belongs to me.'

She had taken off her other glove, unbuttoned her coat and untied the yellow scarf that covered her head. Putting up her hands she smoothed back her hair from her temples. It seemed a deliberate gesture, as though she was preparing herself for my scrutiny. Her face was broad and rather flat, the grey eyes wide-set, her mouth big and soft and all the time smiling. And she was well covered, with big breasts and a plump, round neck that had already folded into little creases. She wore her black hair in a pony tail and, as she leaned back in her chair, she put one hand behind her head and scooped up the long mane so that it fell across her shoulder.

She wasn't particularly pretty, but she had a quality of youth and an exquisite freshness. A little, plump, bountiful Demeter, all generous and ripe. Straightaway I was entranced by her. She was like the first bite into the first summer peach.

Now, you're thinking she was hardly the kind of girl to appeal to me. My women friends have always been sophisticated and shared my interests, at least to some measure. Obviously she wasn't very bright. Her conversation wasn't going to be very stimulating. But flowers don't talk at all, and neither do animals, and we still like to have them near us and look at them. Probably it wouldn't have mattered what she was like. It would have been the same if she had been a completely different kind of woman. She was Doyle's girl.

She smiled and said, 'Why are you staring at me?'

'Isn't that what I'm supposed to be doing?'

She giggled. 'Oh, go on!'

I was thinking that she needed someone to look after

her. She should never have walked like this into a strange man's room. Anything could have happened to her. I might have been a professional seducer or a sex maniac. As for her friendship with Freddy Doyle, it was beyond belief . . .

I said, 'How long have you known Freddy?'

She was just about to answer. She opened her big soft lips, and I could see her pointed pink tongue inside her mouth. Then she stopped and said, 'There you go, asking questions, like Freddy said.'

'Why should he mind? It's just a polite, sociable question.'

Instantly she was quite upset. She couldn't bear the hint of rebuke in my voice. Everything had to be nice, everyone had to be happy. She was the kind of girl who wanted the sun always shining. 'I don't mind,' she assured me. 'It's just that Freddy doesn't like people nosing around in his business. He's one of those quiet ones, you know. You look as if you might be one of those quiet ones yourself.'

I said, 'I'm glad you haven't cut your hair. It suits you like that.'

'Do you think so? I have cut some of it. Half of it's gone. I used to be able to sit on it.'

'Well, then, don't ever cut the rest.'

'You're just like Freddy. That's what he says.'

I said, 'My wife had long black hair, like yours. She was drowned in a storm at sea.'

'Oh, you poor thing. I am sorry.' She had caught sight of my clock on the mantelpiece. 'I say, is that the time? I've got to go.' She threw the scarf over her head and tied it under her chin. 'Can I have it now?'

For some moments I'd been wondering what I was going to say when we got around to this moment. I'd made my little plan. I said, 'I can't let you have it now. It's not here.'

She looked frightened. Her mouth dropped open, and all the light went out of her eyes. 'Oh, no! You don't mean it!'

I said, 'I'll meet you for lunch tomorrow and I'll give it to you then.'

Do you want to know what was going on in my head? I'll tell you.

I'd suspected Doyle of something perverted and frightful. I'd suspected him of having murdered a woman, perhaps because he loved her, and all he could keep and have for himself was this one, imperishable part of her. That's what I had thought.

But now, here was his girl, and there wasn't any guilty secret, only the shame of a simple, sentimental young man who had plundered his sweetheart's head for a souvenir. Here was his girl, alive and complete, come to beg for her own tresses. And everything I'd thought was an illusion, perhaps some eruption from my own mind, some spasm of my own grief. I felt that I had been mad and that now I was sane. Gladys Wilson had brought me back my sanity.

And I said to myself, I'll have you. I had taken Doyle's hank of hair and now I'd take his girl. I made up my mind straightaway. But I knew I would have to go carefully. Obviously she was interested in Doyle. I was going to have to wean her away from him, and that would take time. There were a lot of things I had to find out. Where she lived. What she did. I was quite prepared now to part with the hair. It had no more importance for me. All the mystery that had gathered around it, the enigmatic beauty, and the horror too, all was gone. You might say that I had found something better. I would have given it to her then and there, but I knew that I'd lose her if I did. I needed time, and so I put her off.

Are you thinking that my suspicions were easily dispelled? Of all people you must surely know that there is no limit to the power of self-deception. Where there's a will. And Doyle was clever – he had offered tasty meat to a hungry man. Even so, if you could have seen her as she was on that day – she had upset all my calculations. Even Doyle seemed to shelter behind her. I saw him altered – composed and modified.

She said, 'Well, I don't know. I don't know what to say.'

'Will he be angry with you for going back without it?'

'He might.'

I wondered whether she was upset at the thought of giving him displeasure or because she was afraid of him.

'Tell me where you live.'

She wouldn't do that. She shook her head, bit her lip, looked at the floor. She was almost in tears. 'I never thought you wouldn't,' she burst out. 'You looked so nice.'

'Look, Gladys' – I took her hand – 'I can't imagine anyone not being nice to you. You're so sweet. I don't want you to get into trouble with Freddy over this. You tell him I promised. And you meet me tomorrow.'

'Perhaps, Freddy . . .' She looked at me uncertainly.

'No, not Freddy. If you send Freddy I won't give it to him. I've told him before. What's the matter? Why won't you come? What's wrong with me? Don't you like me?'

She gave me a big radiant smile. 'Of course I like you. You've got a nice face. I like you a lot.'

'Then why won't you meet me tomorrow?'

'I will. I don't see why I shouldn't. I'll give it a try.'

'You don't have to tell him.'

She stood up. 'Oh yes, I'd tell him. I don't keep anything from Freddy.'

'And does he keep anything from you?'

'Of *course* not. What do you think Freddy is?'

I didn't answer her question. I no longer knew what Freddy was. I said, 'Do you live far away? Let me take you home.'

'He wouldn't want you taking me home.'

'Is he waiting for you?'

'I didn't say that.' She sounded stiff and resentful, and I felt I had lost her goodwill. I said, 'I'm sorry, Gladys, please forgive me. It's just that you're so young and pretty, and I don't like the idea of your going out in the dark alone.'

She laughed. 'Oh, go on!'

'Where will we meet tomorrow?'

She considered and then said, 'I'll meet you at one o'clock at the top of the stairs in the South Kensington tube station. Will that be all right? You will bring it?' she added anxiously.

'Of course I will. I promise.'

Like a fool I didn't follow her. I took her downstairs, saw her out of the door and then went back to my room. I wanted to show her that she could trust me.

And she walked off into the dark. A messenger, rejected, empty-handed, taking her failure back to Freddy Doyle.

CHAPTER 10

That evening, sitting on the edge of my bed, I unwrapped the piece of green silk for a last look at the hank of hair, and it seemed to me, as I let it flow over my hand and turned it to the mild light, that some of the life had gone out of it. It looked dull and old. It no longer spoke so insistently to my imagination. The world of reference around it had changed. Once it had conjured up Rachel's drowned face. But looking at it now I thought of Gladys Wilson, sitting in this very room with the light shining on her black hair. How much silkier and glossier than this dull, brittle stuff.

I no longer minded giving it up. And although none of the mystery about it had been solved, I no longer felt intensely curious to know why Doyle, and now Gladys, wanted it so urgently.

I don't mean that I had ceased to be interested in Doyle. Far from it. But the balance of the situation had altered. From the moment that Gladys entered the scene it was natural that the hair should seem unimportant, as though it had been her substitute, reserving a position which she had now stepped forward to claim. And Doyle and I were now in a contest for a different prize. So far all I had to do was to sit passively, guarding my discovery, while he, and then she, invaded my life to try and take it from me. Now the situation was reversed, and it was I who would have to go out after them. It was a very different prospect. I did not know who they were or where they lived, and Doyle had the trump card, which until lately I had held, in his hand.

I wrapped the hair up and put it away. Then I put on my hat and coat and went out. It was about seven-thirty, but I didn't feel like dinner. I was in a peculiar frame of mind.

When I thought of Gladys and our meeting the next day I felt elated, buoyant, excited; then my thoughts slid off her to Doyle, and a feeling of despondency and dread took hold. All that was furtive and unexplained in the affair once more rose up to haunt and puzzle me. I cursed myself for not having found out where she lived and resolved, next time we met, to follow her home.

And so I walked on, turning these thoughts over and over in my head. Doyle, Gladys . . . how had they met, how long had they known one another, how intimate were they? Were they sleeping together? The notion was hideous, and the very thought made my skin damp and cold with horror. But surely it was probable? Demeter the bountiful, and the mongrel beast.

I found myself down by the river and walked along, looking out over the water. It was a cold night, and there weren't many people about. The wind rattled the grimy, blackened leaves of laurels in the street plantations; the reflections of lights hung in unstable, liquid splashes on the water.

Several times lately I had taken this walk. I had grown to

enjoy my solitude. I liked to look out of it and contemplate the city at night. All the lighted rooms, the meals being cooked, the beds, the embracing couples. All that enormous complex edifice of buildings and streets and interior decoration providing a cover for desires and fears. All that for warmth and bread and to guard against the cry of the wolf. It was an awe-inspiring thought, too big for me. I felt that night that I could hardly endure my loneliness. I felt afraid, not of anything following me or threatening me, but of something that seemed to have taken up residence within me. Some knowledge, as yet half unveiled.

I saw the lights of a pub shining through the engraved glass of its windows. Inside, the blurred pink shapes of faces ... smoke and talk ... I turned towards it to escape from my thoughts.

The place was jammed full. You could hardly see for smoke. Everyone was shrieking. Every time you moved you trod on someone or slopped someone's glass of beer.

I pushed my way to the bar, got shoved in the back and fell on an elbow just as the owner of it was draining his glass. He choked and turned round to tell me what he thought of me.

'Sorry,' I said, 'someone shoved me in the back.'

'Well, by Jove!' It was Sinclair, frothy around the moustache and baggy under the eyes. He looked as if he had had quite a few. And beside him, actually within his encircling tweed sleeve, was Peggy. She'd been drinking too, but it didn't have the same effect on her country girl complexion, just gave her a high colour and made her giggly. She was nuzzling her little snub nose into the shoulder of his coat.

At the sight of me she pushed back and tried to look as if she didn't know him.

He looked as if he wished he didn't know her either. Only it was a bit difficult, because he had forgotten to take his arm away, and she was still clasped to his manly bosom. I could see his thoughts spinning away behind his glassy humourless eyes. I could see him deciding to brazen it out and make the best of it.

'My dear chap! Glad you turned up. Jolly glad to see you!'

It dawned on me that I must be in the Three Bells – the pub by the river, that wasn't 'too close to home'.

The Major knuckled his moustache. 'What's your particular brand of poison?'

I said that a bitter would do.

He bawled at the barmaid, calling her 'Sweetie' and letting me see that he knew her well.

Peggy pulled down her sweater and patted her hair. She was wearing pale blue and a lot of shiny beads around her neck, obviously dressed up for a night out. She had on an excessively heady perfume. I liked her better in the tight uniform with the safety pin. For some reason I hated to see her there, pawed by the Major and swilling beer. It struck me suddenly that she resembled Gladys.

She obviously hated to see me too. 'I think I'll just go and powder my nose,' she said and started to push her way unsteadily through the crowd to the door of the Ladies near the end of the bar.

The Major gave me a jolt with his elbow. 'Had a few,' he remarked in a succulent voice.

I said, 'She's running away from me.'

He gaped and began to stutter.

'Didn't you know she let Doyle into my room?'

'Good God! Good God!' He said it over and over again, and his eyes were as round as marbles. 'You mean she let him in . . .'

'For that thing he was looking for in the davenport.'

'Those filthy postcards . . .'

'That's right.'

Of course he knew all about it. He'd told her to do it himself, or told her not to interfere. I was amused at the way he overplayed his astonishment. I wondered what power Doyle had over him to be able to talk him into such an embarrassing position. Women, I supposed. There must have been other Peggys – a whole string of them. Do as I say, or I'll talk to your wife . . . I had suspected for a long time that it was Mrs Sinclair who had the money, prob-ably Mrs Sinclair who owned the hotel. Otherwise, why on earth would he have married her? He was on a lovely wicket. She paid all the bills, did all the work and he had all the fun. Only she was puritanical and vindictive, and his sort of fun would have upset her if she'd known about it.

'I say, old chap!' He leaned so close to me I could see the hairs of his moustache trembling with his beery breath. 'I'd be most frightfully obliged if you wouldn't say anything to the wife.'

'Doesn't she know you're here?'

He looked thoroughly insulted for a moment and said stiffly, 'Don't have to answer to the wife for every drink I like to have. I mean Peggy, old chap. I mean Peggy going into your room with Doyle.'

'I didn't say she went into my room with Doyle. I said she let him in.'

'What's that?' He pretended not to hear, and there was an awful din going on around us. 'What I mean is, it's like this, if my wife knew there was something a bit, you know, a bit not quite right going on, she'd get rid of Peggy on the spot. Wouldn't like that, would we?' He twirled his moustache. 'Nice little thing.'

'Well, if she goes around showing strangers into your guests' bedrooms . . .'

'Beggars can't be choosers. Can't get girls for love or money. My wife would be down on her knees cleaning the stairs herself. That's what she'd be doing. Cutting off her nose to spite her face. Can't have that. May's a bit of an invalid. Not too well.'

He leaned forward again. 'I say, you didn't find them, did you?'

'What?'

'Those pornographic pictures.'

'No, I didn't find them.'

'Funny thing. He must have been sure they were there.'

I said, 'You got to know Doyle quite well, didn't you? What does he do for a living?'

But he shut up like a clam. 'Can't tell you, old man. Can't tell you a thing about him. Used to run into him having a pint now and again.'

'No forwarding address?'

'Just disappeared. Didn't see him again until that day, you know, when he turned up and kicked up that shemozzle about his you know what.'

I bought him a beer and, as he drank it, he took my goodwill for granted. 'Much obliged to you, old man. Much obliged. Don't like keeping things from the wife, you know, but anything for a quiet life.'

Peggy was coming back. I said, 'Well, I'll be off. I won't spoil your evening.'

He was expansive with gratitude. 'Much obliged to you, old man. Why don't we make a night of it sometime?' He lowered his voice. 'You know I've got this little place down in Essex. Like to get away for the weekends. Wife doesn't like the country. Why don't you come down? Got a little bit of something lined up? I'll bet you have, you dog! Bring her along. Rather enjoy a foursome. If you get sick of what you've brought along yourself, we can always swap, eh? Ha! Ha!'

He was still laughing when I got to the door and pushed my way out into the night.

I felt better after that. Strange how the display of a little power gives us back our confidence. I'd caught the Major in an embarrassing moment. I had shaken my fist discreetly in his face and then shown mercy. I felt ready to tackle Doyle all over again.

All that was changed was that my certainty was shaken. I no longer knew what kind of a man it was I was dealing with. I had been certain before, but Gladys had upset my calculations. There had to be some tenderness in Doyle to account for Gladys. That was the way I looked at it.

What I did not consider was that there might be something in Gladys to account for Doyle.

CHAPTER 11

I was first to arrive, and I looked in all the shop windows while I waited for her; the florists and the tobacconists on one side of the station arcade and the carpet shop and the bookstall on the other. I bought a paper and read that the police were looking for another missing girl, a twelve-year-old who had left her home on a Saturday afternoon to stay with friends but had never arrived. There had been a lot of these cases lately.

Twice I went around the shops, and the second time I passed the carpet shop. There she was at the top of the steps. Out of breath, having hurried, so she said, being five minutes late.

She only had an hour. She had to get back to work. What work? I asked. She wouldn't tell me. Did I have it? Yes, I did – wrapped in brown paper and stuffed in my overcoat pocket.

Where would she like to have lunch?

Somewhere close, because she only had an hour.

I took her to a place called the Bamboo Bar, where you get rice, chicken and pork. Not Chinese cooking, but a kind of compromise leaning toward it. I thought she might like it, and she did.

It was full of Chinese and Thais and a few French students who couldn't bear to eat in English restaurants. We sat at a table against the wall, looking across at some Chinese embroidered panels. 'I like this,' she said eagerly. 'I like this sort of place.'

Didn't Freddy bring her to places like this? No, not often. It turned out that Freddy preferred eating at home. He liked little things she cooked up for him on the gas ring. Sausage and chips, fried eggs – things like that. Only she bought the chips already cooked at the fish shop on the corner, from which I concluded that they probably lived in the same boarding-house. Not a private hotel like the Sinclairs', who would never have allowed sausages and chips cooked on a gas ring, but something a bit lower in the social grade. And I wondered why Freddy had gone from the comfort of the Sinclairs' to live in such a place, when he obviously had the money to live better.

Had he perhaps met Gladys and gone to live in her boarding house to be near her? Or had he gone there first and then met her? Had he gone to such a place with the idea of meeting, not necessarily Gladys, but a girl like Gladys?

She told me quite a lot about him, without knowing it. She couldn't help giving herself away. There was no deceit in her, and people without deceit can't detect it in anyone else, so she never understood that I was cross-examining her.

What she told me about Doyle was, briefly, that to her, as to everyone else, he was a bit of a mystery. A close, secretive man. A man who did not like people prying into his affairs. Who came and went and accounted to nobody, not even to her. 'Oh! He's got plenty of money!' Proudly . . . but she didn't know where he got it. He had some job or other. A job in town, an awfully good job, because he could get off whenever he wanted. He didn't do regular hours like you do in an office or a shop. And he had his own car. He just went around in that whenever he felt like it.

It was as I had suspected. He didn't do anything at all. Like myself, he had leisure. That most precious, that most desirable of all blessings that everyone wants and nearly everyone abuses.

The place was crowded, and we had a table for four, but nobody came to take the other two seats. I put the paper package containing the hank of hair down on one of them, and neither of us looked at it or bothered about it throughout that hour from one until two.

She said she didn't want much to eat because she was dieting, but she ended up by having quite a lot. And she really tucked in. She was a little glutton. When the Chinese part of the meal was finished she wanted something sweet, and finding there was an occidental side to the menu card, ordered an ice-cream, a mixed-up multicoloured thing with a cherry on top. She devoured it greedily, like a child at a picnic. I felt I should tell her not to betray so openly all that rapture over a mere ice-cream. A man at the table next to us was watching her with heavy speculative eyes. She was quite unaware of him.

Women had looked at Doyle because of his beauty, and men looked at Gladys seeing something seductive in her innocence.

When she had finished, she put down her spoon and looked up and said, 'I *did* enjoy that!'

'Good,' I said. 'I can't think of anything nicer than giving you pleasure. We must come again.'

I could see that she was pleased. A smile came into the corners of her lips, and she couldn't manage to get rid of it. She was very young, and the attentions of a man so much older than her must have flattered her. But she said, 'Oh, I couldn't do that. Freddy said just this once. I couldn't come again. He wouldn't like it.'

'And what about me? Don't I deserve some compassion?'

She giggled and lowered her eyes. 'Oh, you'll be all right.'

'I mean it.' I leaned over the table towards her. Her hand was lying there and I put mine upon it. I said, 'I'm very lonely. Since my wife died I haven't any friends. Not anyone at all. If I could see you sometimes, it would mean a great deal to me.'

She was so sorry for me I'll swear there were tears in her eyes. 'I am sorry,' she began.

'After all, why not? Freddy doesn't own you. You may be his girl, but that doesn't mean you can't have other friends.'

I know she wanted to say yes. She was soft and bursting with pity. She must have been afraid of him and, not wanting to put her on a wrack of indecision, I dropped the subject. I said, 'I like your dress. Is it new?'

It was awful. A pink thing of just the wrong colour, with frills at the neck. It was so awful that a kind of compassion for her compelled me to praise it.

She brightened up. 'I made it myself. I always make all my own.'

'What a wonderful wife you'll make for some lucky man.'

'Oh, I don't know, I've got an awful temper.'

'Will it be Freddy?'

She frowned and for a moment I thought she was going to confide in me. 'I love Freddy, but he's not a family man. I think I'd like a family man. Heavens!' She had seen the clock. 'I've got to go. I've only got five minutes. I'll have to tear. I'll have to run all the way. My boss is so fussy about us girls being on time.'

Again she had told me a great deal. That she worked nearby, within walking distance, or running distance at any rate, of the Bamboo Bar. And that other girls worked there too.

Outside on the pavement she paused to tie her scarf under her throat. There was a little grass plantation in the middle of the road, which in spring was bright with tall tulips, and a man sat huddled on a wooden seat feeding pigeons.

Somebody touched my arm. 'Did you leave this behind?' He spoke with an accent – German I think. It was the man at the next table who had been watching Gladys. A square, squat individual with podgy white hands. He gave me the precious parcel, nodded, looked at Gladys again and waddled off.

'Fancy forgetting that! Well, what do you know?' She laughed.

'Well, there you are.'

I couldn't withhold it any longer. I had given her my promise. She took it from me, casually at first, but just as she could not hide her greed for ice-creams, so now she could not disguise her interest and surprise.

I saw her feeling its strange, slithery softness in her fingers, and her face was rumpled and enquiring, like the face of a child trying to guess the contents of a Christmas parcel.

Suddenly I understood. 'Aren't you going to open it?' I asked.

'No, why should I?'

'It isn't what you thought it was going to be, is it?'

'I didn't think . . .' She bit her lip.

'You didn't think anything. You didn't know what it was. You've been lying to me!'

'I haven't! I haven't!' She was nearly in tears.

'You said it was yours!' I was furious with her. I took her by the shoulders and shook her, there in the street, as we both stood.

'What's his is mine!'

She was scared to death – first of him, and now of me. She saw my face, and her own face was contorted with terror. She snatched herself out of my hands and began to run.

I ran after her, but only a step or two. There was a pub on the corner, and he must have been standing in the doorway, watching us. I hadn't thought to keep a lookout for him, though later, when I looked back on the incident, my own naivety astounded me. He must have been watching us through every moment. He would never have allowed our meeting to have passed unscrutinised.

He only had to dart forward and stick out his foot, and I was over it and sprawling. I flung out my hands, but not before I had cracked my head on the pavement and almost lost my senses for a moment or two. When the world stopped spinning round he was standing over me, gently digging me in the ribs with his toe, looking down and grinning. It was the only time I ever saw him looking really good-natured.

I got to my feet and brushed myself down. I was still dizzy, and his face quivered in front of me and broke apart and multiplied, like a face in a nightmare. I said, 'You've left me no alternative.'

He had his teeth clenched and his lips drawn back. I suppose you could call it a smile. He stood with his feet a little apart and his hands hanging at his sides as though they were things he had no use for.

'No alternative,' I repeated, trying to force him into asking a question.

'What do you mean?'

'Now I'll have to go to the police.'

I heard a faint sound, like the hiss of a snake. But his expression didn't change. 'You're kidding. You wouldn't do that.'

He spoke with the utmost confidence, as though from some deeply considered certainty, as though he knew something about me that I didn't know myself. 'You won't do that,' he said again and turned and walked away from me down the street. I knew there was no point in following him. He would simply lead me on some wild goose chase until eventually he had thrown me off.

And so I lost them both, lost everything I had.

CHAPTER 12

I began walking down the pavement towards the tube station hardly knowing what I was doing or where I was going. I reached the corner where an old man was selling chrysanthemums and stood there, looking around me vaguely. I felt stunned, though I confess that at first I was wrapped up in my personal loss rather than afraid for Gladys.

For nearly three weeks my life had revolved around Doyle and my hank of hair. I had been living in a confined, intense little world that had worked my nerves into a pitch of excitement and expectation. Then Gladys came, like a culmination, the cryptic promise implied from the first.

And then, as suddenly, nothing. They had gone, and I did not know where to look for them. I felt like the knight in 'La Belle Dame sans Merci' who wakes to find the fairy has disappeared. It wasn't grief I felt but something more painful, like a sudden, agonising starvation.

I wandered up the Old Brompton Road in a nightmare of boredom and distress. As I walked I glanced vaguely into the shop windows, into an interior decorator's full of striped damask and Chinese porcelain jars converted into lamps. I passed a shop that sold artists' materials and had a dreadful picture in the window. Two men were carrying a wardrobe in through the door of an auction room. In any of these places Gladys might be working. But I wasn't consciously looking for her then. I was just stumbling along, impelled by my aching thoughts, tasting my own loss.

Later that evening, back in my room, I faced the situation more sensibly and formed my resolution. There was only one thing to do. I had to go out and look for her. I had to walk through every street and into every office and shop in the vicinity. Somehow I had to find her. I told myself it shouldn't be difficult. She had had five minutes in which to run from the Bamboo Bar. Cover an area within a five-minute running distance of a given point in London. Or in a case of miscalculation make it ten minutes. Not difficult at all. Not at all. Just try it some time.

The first day I quite enjoyed myself. I had something to do again, somewhere to go. I set about my search with a grim, dedicated determination, and for the whole day tramped along those grey, reticent streets.

Between twelve and one I tried every café and espresso bar. I went back to the Bamboo Bar, thinking she might have liked it and returned. I even went and stood at the top of the steps in the tube station, feeling that these places had some special claim on her.

By five o'clock, my mind was rioting with weird fancies. I told myself that by now surely she must be afraid and that she would turn to me as her protector. I even told myself that Doyle would find it impossible to sever the bond that had been forged between us and that he would return to the places we had been in together, if only to gloat over my defeat. I had a cup of tea in the café with the red Formica tables and ate a sandwich made of bone-white bread. I remembered his waxy hands on the red table, and I longed and yearned for him no less than Gladys.

At five o'clock I went up to the Print Room, thinking perhaps she would be there. I had told her how I spent every day in the Print Room. It would be the logical place for her to look for me, or perhaps Doyle would go there to spy on me.

They were just closing up. There was no one there except the two attendants and my Hittite girl, wearing green woollen stockings, a chunky black sweater and the bronze necklace. The young attendant with the spiky hair greeted me warmly, as though a feeling of friendship he had not known about before had grown and strengthened in my absence. 'We've missed you, Mr Hand. We wondered if you'd caught this beastly flu.'

And my Hittite girl gave me a quick half smile.

The Print Room galleries were again open to the public, and I walked with her down the stairs past the stained-glass window to the Italian Renaissance. It was the first time we had spoken to each other. She told me her name was Myra Cohen. I said, 'Did you happen to notice today if a plump dark girl with long black hair came into the Print Room?'

No, she was pretty sure that no one like that had come in.

'Or a handsome man in good clothes? Thirtyish. He has a long face and a lot of thick, wavy hair. And peculiar eyes.'

She said he might have come in, but she hadn't noticed.

'You would have noticed if he had,' I said. 'Women always do.'

She said that she wasn't 'women'. She was herself.

Suddenly I longed to tell her everything about Doyle and Gladys and the hank of hair. Something told me that she would listen to me sympathetically and would neither laugh nor ask questions. She was an artist, even if a bad one. She moved in an artist's world. 'I am not 'women' – I am myself . . .' She understood eccentricity, cherished it. She would not be bemused by my odd behaviour.

For you understand that this was why I could not go to the police. I knew I ought to. With every moment that passed, the threat to Gladys appeared more monstrous and immediate. Terror awaited her, horror, and a dreadful death. I predicted her fate with an ever-increasing certainty. And only I had the power to save her.

I should go to the police! I knew! But I felt a shrinking dread of exposing myself to the scrutiny of ordinary, unimaginative men. Doyle had known that. Doyle had understood that my thoughts were as strange and as secretive as his. He counted on my keeping the contest personal between us.

'I catch a bus here,' Myra said.

'Well, I'll say goodbye.'

I was glad to have talked to her and, as I turned away, felt in some small degree comforted. It is ironic to think of this now. I said to myself, There is a woman I might have loved, one of my own kind.

Next day it was the same again. The same streets, the same shops, the same cafés. But I went further afield, stretching that five minutes to eight and ten.

It was a cold, obscure day, with a hint of fog giving tenderness to the outlines of the buildings around me. Each shop and coffee bar looked promising by the very warmth of light in the windows. Heat and fire to keep the wolf away . . . But nothing. Nothing. Only strange faces, unwelcoming eyes.

By four o'clock the reiterated stab of disappointment had reduced my spirit to a spongy wound. They had gone, they had disappeared into a secrecy and silence as complete as death.

There was only one thing to do and, by now, I had brought myself to the point of seriously considering it. You, of course, will have your own ideas why I had hesitated for so long. I had wandered far from the Bamboo Bar. You would have had to have been an Olympic runner to have covered the distance in five minutes. I got on a bus to take me back to South Kensington.

I sat upstairs in a window seat, and a small boy with dirty knees sniffed and wriggled incessantly beside me. Two middle-aged women were sitting in front, with shopping baskets on their laps. One wore a blue scarf round her head and the other a curious black hat pierced by a silver pin that had a green glass bead on the end.

I kept looking at this head, that twinkled when she moved her head to talk to her friend. I felt exhausted and frightened of the oncoming dark, of the cigarette butts on the floor, of the silver pin in the woman's hat. And, as I sat there, nursing my fear, it seemed to swell and burst within me, out of my skin, until it was like a hot, suffocating substance buttoned up between my body and my overcoat.

The two women in front of me were talking loudly, and, to control my fear, to give it some point of focus, and thereby diminish and contain it, I listened to what they were saying.

'You'd think she'd fall to bits when they pulled her out,' said the woman with the blue scarf. 'How on earth would they be able to tell who she was?'

'Their skins are darker than ours, you know,' said the woman with the pin in her hat.

'You wouldn't think there'd be much difference after all that time. You wouldn't think she'd have a skin and, if she did, wouldn't it be sort of purple?'

'They can tell by the teeth.'

'Imagine them not finding her before. Down a well for five weeks. You'd think they'd have smelt her.'

'Well, it was awfully cut off,' said the woman with the pin in her hat. 'Right down at the bottom of the garden. You wouldn't have any cause to be going down to the bottom of the garden, not in this weather. And it had a lid on it.'

'The well . . .'

'Yes, it had a wooden lid. It said so in the paper. Nobody ever went near it. That was good luck for the chap that did it, wasn't it?'

They had begun to collect their shopping baskets and struggled to their feet. The wriggling boy sitting next to me belonged to them, for his hand was clutched and he was hoisted to his feet by the woman with the blue scarf.

'Terrible, I call it. Just terrible. And her a foreigner. All that way from home, though, mind you, I expect worse things happen out there in India. They make you lie down on nails, those religious men. And they bury you up to the head in the earth. It's all part of their religion.'

'I don't mind a nice clean murder,' said the woman with pins in her hair. 'Crime passional and all that, you know. If you ask me, some girls are just asking for it. But fancy going and cutting off a piece of her hair like that. What would he want it for? To add to his collection, if you ask me. Makes your blood run cold.'

CHAPTER 13

I was down on the floor and I was struggling to get up. I was retching and horrified with myself, thinking that I mustn't be sick in the bus. I mustn't disgrace myself. I must hang on at all costs and present myself to the public as an ordinary decent man. There I was, struggling away on the floor, among the boots and stockings and the frightening filthy crushed-out ends of cigarettes. And perhaps people were thinking, He has fits . . . maybe he's dangerous!

'I'm perfectly all right,' I said.

But they were crowding around me, and someone said, 'Give him air.'

Someone else said, 'Put his head between his knees . . .'

The woman with the blue scarf was leaning down to get a good look.

And the boy was there too. I could smell his sweaty boy smell. Not unpleasant. Not at all unpleasant.

I would have been able to get up if they hadn't been leaning around and helping me. I was like a body dropped in a well, and how can you get up if all the faces are stuck in the top, shutting out the light, guzzling the air.

I could hear someone sobbing. Someone else said, 'I think he's having a fit.'

Then the conductor helped me up. I could see the big silver buttons on his uniform. Or were they brass? Silver, brass, silver, brass. Which was it? Does it matter? Silver is a precious metal. Thieves will rob for silver and hit innocent women on the head or knife them in the belly and then cut them up into small pieces and put them into incinerators. Except the hair. You keep the hair. You keep it to show what you've done. You keep it for triumph and joy, to live and re-live the dreadful deed. The last of your love, the passive, imperishable part that cannot reject or refuse, or do anything at all. You keep that.

Then I was out on the pavement lying flat on my back and looking up at the grey, solemn sky and the big grey houses, all closed up on their human lives like tombstones confining the already dead. We are all already dead. I know that's banal. Please forgive me. This part of what happened, the revelation, you see, the dreadful moment when all my fears were admitted into my consciousness, this always excites me.

Doyle had murdered a woman and stuffed her body down a well. And he had cut the hair from her head and hidden it in my davenport. I had always known. Right from the beginning when I dropped it on the floor, feeling the sting of terror still electric in those tresses.

He had cut off a piece of living fear to keep for himself. And then he had gone away to look for another woman – any woman, providing she was incautious and endowed for mutilation.

So I lay on the pavement, thinking, We are all already dead. And as we all have to die anyway, isn't it a privilege to die violently at the hand of a desiring man, who, having killed you, keeps you for himself – for joy forever. Not a bad death, I'd say. Better than dying of cancer or leprosy. Or loneliness. As the tightening fingers choked the life out of your throat, at least you could say to yourself, 'Someone cared!'

Look at me, think of me. If I had died there, lying on my back on the pavement, from that vast indifferent city would have sounded not one sigh.

Someone said, 'If he sat up and put his head between his knees . . .' And I thought, A good idea, I'll try that. I tried it, looking now not at the sky, but at the damp grey pavement.

'Are you all right now, sir?' It was the conductor again. He had stopped the bus, and there it was, the big red brute of a thing grunting away, and every eye in it turned upon me.

'I'm perfectly all right,' I said. 'Leave me alone! I'm all right!' And I got up and began to lurch about a bit, trying to get my balance.

'Here, hang on to me.' But I got away from him and was off down the footpath, looking down to see where I was putting my feet. And I thought to myself, I mustn't tread on any of the lines, because if I tread on a line that means he's killed her. And for the space of thirty seconds her fate was in my feet.

'Hey! Look out!' They were still worrying about me and hurrying along beside me. The damned woman with that silver pin and the poisonous green bead. And I rammed my head straight into a tall, comfortable, stolid London bobby.

'Watch where you're going, sir!'

'He's ill. He fainted on the bus!'

'Someone ought to take him home!'

Everyone giving advice, telling him what he ought to do.

I said, 'Officer! I want to go to a police station. I want to report a crime.'

'Well, sir . . .'

I shouted at him. 'I have information about a crime!'

CHAPTER 14

I knew how it would be. That was why I hadn't been to see them. I knew exactly how it would be. And that's how it was.

I liked the bobby best. He was big and gentle, and he didn't pretend to understand. Then there were two of them, asking me questions and writing things down. They were stolid, calm, completely unsurprised. I had the impression that nothing was too strange for them.

They took me into an inner office and there were two plain-clothes men, Sergeant Heath and Inspector Cunningham. Heath was a sharp man with an intelligent, batlike face. Big mouth, big ears, big, wide-awake eyes. Cunningham was heavy and thick, all the nerves in his face covered up under flesh. He sat back in his chair in an unchanging aura of disbelief, and nothing struck any reaction. Nothing at all. After a while I talked to Heath, seeing the reflections of my words in that keen, bat face.

They were interested in what I was saying. Naturally. But they didn't either of them like me much. Though they treated me kindly enough. They offered me a cigarette, made me sit in a comfortable chair. They ordered a cup of tea. They told me to calm myself, to be quiet for a moment and compose my thoughts. I shouted at them, 'How can I compose my thoughts? Don't you understand, this girl is in danger! If she's not already dead.'

Yes, they had gathered that I was worried about the safety of a girl. They had taken her name. Gladys Wilson. Was I sure that this was her correct name? Would she by any chance have any reason to give a false name?

Yes, I had to admit it. She might have a very good reason for giving me a false name.

And what would that reason be?

'He might have told her to,' I said. 'He took a risk in sending her to me, and he must have wanted to protect himself, so I suppose he told her to give me a false name.'

Ah, yes. They glanced at one another, then at my hands, which were trembling and wringing and clasping one another on my lap. I put them in my pockets. That was when they offered me a cigarette.

'No, thank you. Yes, yes. I will.'

'Now, sir, perhaps you can tell us, just exactly why you suspect this man Doyle.'

Struck by a sudden doubt, I said, 'That's the name they gave me at the hotel. That's the name he was known by.'

'But it might not be his name?'

'It might not. He wouldn't be likely to use his real name, would he? He might have a dozen names.'

'Then you think it was premeditated, Mr Hand?'

'Not necessarily. No. I don't expect it would be premeditated in the sense you mean. It would be more of a compulsion . . .'

'But you think he probably used an assumed name . . .'

I burst out, 'I thought you police weren't interested in what people think. I thought it was facts you were after.'

'Well, sir, that's true. But up-to-date all we've had from you is suppositions. We'd be glad to have a few facts. We'd be really grateful.' That was Cunningham. Without a muscle moving. Without the twitch of a nerve.

And then I told them about the hair in the davenport. 'That's a fact for you,' I said. 'That's a fact! This man Doyle had that room before me. He tried to get into it again secretly, he tried to get Sinclair to open it up and let him in, and then, when Sinclair refused, he broke in and searched it for himself. I caught him at it and he attacked me, only I got the better of him. Those are facts for you . . . plenty of facts!'

'Very peculiar facts.' That was Heath and he was looking at me as if I were another peculiar fact.

I said, 'She may be dead. It's two days since I saw her. She may be dead.'

I heard my own voice, dull and muffled in that dreary little room. The air seemed thick and padded with the breath of a hundred other interrogations.

'You have a special interest in this girl?'

'No special interest,' came in the same heavy voice. I listened to it and said to myself, No, that's not true. Of course! Of course! 'She's a human being!' I cried. 'A young girl, and this man's a monster!'

Heath said, 'We understand your anxiety. We understand. We're doing everything we can.'

'This woman they found down the well, some women were talking about her on top of the bus. I am right, aren't I? There isn't a mistake about that? He had cut away some of the hair off the side of her head . . .'

'Yes, sir, that's correct. Some of her hair had been cut off.'

'And it was long and black. That's right, isn't it? It was long black hair.'

'When you said you knew something about that crime, Mr Hand, we checked to get all the details we could. The report is still not complete, but we do know that she had long black hair and that some of it had been cut off.'

'What else do you know?'

'She was put down a disused well in the bottom of a cottage garden. Some children found her. From a nearby farm. There was no one in the cottage. It's a weekend place. Monday to Friday it's shut up and empty.'

'Do you know who it belongs to?'

I was talking to Heath. I saw his eyes become wary and sharp. 'Now, if you'd just carry on with your story, sir. We can't give you a lot of information yet. As I say, the report's not complete.'

Cunningham said, 'One curious aspect of your story, Mr Hand, is this. If this man Doyle is our murderer, it is surely inconceivable that he would return to the hotel and try to get hold of evidence that could convict him. He would have been much safer to have left it where it was. You say it was well hidden away. He had no reason to believe that anyone had found it. It could have stayed there for years. The best thing that he could have done would have been to have left it where it was. Never go near the place again. He behaved like a madman. He gave himself away. If he's our man.'

His stupidity infuriated me. You couldn't explain Doyle with that kind of reasoning. 'He wanted it,' I told him patiently. 'He murdered this girl to get it, and he wanted it back. Don't you understand?'

'I don't understand at all.' In fact, of course, he did. He wasn't as unimaginative as he looked, and many times before he must have brushed against the Doyles of this world. He understood, all right. What interested him was that I understood too.

I said, 'Women find him attractive, but when they get to know him better he frightens them. Perhaps this is the only way he can keep them . . .'

I broke off . . . seeing the way they looked at each other.

An alarm clock ticked on the desk. I looked at it, and the plain black figures set around its white face seemed to declare with too stark a cruelty the relentless movement of time towards the future.

I said, 'We're sitting here. She may be dead.'

Cunningham leaned forward. 'Why would he want to kill her, Mr Hand?'

'For the same reason he killed the other one.'

'You know what that reason is?'

They both sat, motionless, intent. It wasn't Doyle they were trying to understand, it was me. I said, 'Yes, I know what that reason is.'

But how could I know? That was what they asked themselves. Two very different types of men. Cunningham, detached, calm. He must have seen many strange sights, he must have known many strange and pathetic people. They were the puzzles of his little world, the problems to be solved, that was all. Not so Heath. To Heath they were human beings to hate and to pity. To save, outwit or destroy. Heath was one of them. There was something of Doyle in Heath, something of Sinclair, something of me. At any moment he could become one of us. And he was looking at me and thinking, You are Doyle. You are Doyle.

I could see the thought in his eyes. He was a man of imagination.

A woman is murdered, stuffed down a well. Miles away, weeks ago. Words spoken in a crowd, and the poor dark mind erupts and spews out its fears. Dreads and desires, guilts and repressions. The dark brain articulate in imagination. You are Doyle, he was thinking. You have the whole plot worked out as though you were its creator. He looked at me and I saw pity in his eyes.

It is shocking to be pitied. I had been near to hysteria, but in the face of that unjust pity I grew calm.

Cunningham said, 'Your explanations are interesting. But most men . . .'

But I am not 'most men'. I am myself. I said, 'I have had a lot of time to think about this.'

'If you were afraid for the girl' – this was Heath – 'why didn't you come to us two days ago when you lost track of her?'

'Because of what you are now thinking.'

They saw that if I was mad I was at least not raving. They even looked uncomfortable. I told them how I'd tried to find her and the clue she'd given me that made me think she worked nearby.

Cunningham made a note on a pad. 'That may be of

some help to us.' I had the feeling that he believed he had at last acquired a piece of information. His sort of information. But Doyle did not deal in his sort of information.

Heath said, 'But if you were worried about her, may I ask, Mr Hand, why you gave it back to her?'

'He sent her like a hostage. I had to give it back.'

'Or else he'd knock her around,' said Heath.

'I don't know. Not that exactly. I don't know. I wasn't interested in it any more.'

'Just a minute. What do you mean, you weren't interested in it any more? Just what kind of interest did you have in it?'

'I didn't have any interest. I don't know what you mean. It was a mystery. I am interested in mysteries.'

'But when you gave it back you hadn't solved the mystery, had you? So why weren't you interested any more?'

Because of Gladys. Because of her. You are Doyle.

I said, 'I thought it was hers. She told me that she'd cut her hair. She said it used to be so long she could sit on it.'

'So when you say she was a hostage . . .' That was Heath.

And at the same time Cunningham said, 'Mr Hand, I don't know whether you realise it but you're making some very contradictory statements.'

And so on and so on. I don't know how long. Perhaps another hour. I don't remember what I said. Things that I had never dreamed I had ever thought.

There were interruptions, telephone calls. And one of the policemen came in with a note in his hand.

I said, 'I've told you all I know. I'm exhausted and hungry. I'd like to go now.'

The clock on the desk said seven. They brought me a sandwich.

A little later the policeman came in again with another note, and Cunningham read it and then passed it to Heath.

It was something that had shocked them, I could tell that, not from Cunningham – I had given up expecting anything from Cunningham – but from Heath. The way he swung those big bat eyes like searchlights onto my face. Then he looked at Cunningham and Cunningham nodded.

'We have just received some news, Mr Hand, that I think we can pass on to you. It does seem as if it might support your story. The well where the body was found belonged to a cottage – we already knew that. We now know that the owner of the cottage was a man named Major Derek Sinclair. This could be the Major Sinclair who owns your hotel.'

'His name is Derek.' It wasn't triumph I felt, but despair. She was dead. She was certainly dead.

'Did you know he owned a weekend cottage?'

'He told me about it.'

'You've never been there?'

'Never. He said it was in Essex. He went down last weekend, and the weekend before that.'

'Did he ever take Doyle?'

'I don't know. He must have, mustn't he? He knew him. Some time he must have taken Doyle.'

'The other thing we've learned is that the murdered woman was Indian. And she was dressed in a silk sari. Have you any idea who she could be?'

I knew, but I was tired of them now. Let them ask

someone else. Miss Sacksena, whose friend had gone away to Birmingham and had known Doyle, who might have dropped hairpins in his room. Miss Sacksena could tell them all about her Indian friend. Or Mrs Sinclair or Mrs Pride or even Peggy. But the other questions, the Doyle questions, only I could answer. For only I knew.

I got up, and they made no attempt to stop me. I said, 'It's too late, isn't it? It's all over.'

'There's no reason to assume that, Mr. Hand,' said Heath, and his tone was different now that it began to look as if there was a Doyle. Not just me. Not just the Doyle in me, but another Doyle. 'He'll read the papers. Perhaps he'll become frightened and go into hiding.'

I corrected him. 'He'll read the papers and he'll realise that if he doesn't do it now he may never get a chance. He'll be caught and put in jail, and then he will have lost his chance.'

There they were, thinking again, Doesn't he know a lot about Doyle?

And then I told them all I knew, the very last and most important thing I knew. I said, 'He'll do it again, even if he knows he's going to be caught. What you don't realise is that that lock of hair was the most important thing he possessed, more important than his own safety. Nothing else had any value. And getting it was the most important act of his life.'

We are nothing without love. We are deaf and mute and blind. We are nothing without love. Only I didn't tell them that, although it was what I was thinking. We both knew that, Doyle and me.

CHAPTER 15

I don't know whether they set anyone to follow me. I never thought to ask them – a pity, it would be interesting to know. I was unaware of being followed, then or later. I walked out into the dark streets and, to any detached observer I must have seemed like the loneliest man on earth. Yet I had my thoughts, the incessant throb of fear and desire binding me like a chain to that imperilled girl.

I didn't think where I was going. I didn't think that I was going anywhere or doing anything, yet I made my way back home like a lost dog. There was nothing to do now that the police were looking for Doyle but wait and suffer the end.

I saw it all. I lived through it all down the long pavements, making my way back. Now I trod on all the lines, destroying her deliberately at every step. To get the whole thing over, to shorten her agony. There wasn't a doubt, a hope or a fear that I didn't experience for her, and there wasn't a thought in his brain that I didn't have too. There wasn't a movement he made that I didn't make. It was as clear as crystal. I heard the words he spoke, and the voice of his conscience, like the voice of my own soul. Why shouldn't I know all this? Heath was right. I was

Doyle. From the beginning I understood him, like my twin brother. It had been useless telling the police, for only I knew what was going to happen and only I could prevent it.

When I got back to the hotel I noticed an extraordinary thing. The front door was open. And in the hall all the lights were burning – the main centre light in the middle of the hall, two light brackets with pendant crystals, and a fourth light further down at the end, where the hall led to the kitchens. As though suddenly someone had felt afraid of the dark. In my three week's stay in the hotel I had never known such a thing.

The Sinclairs' door was open. I glanced inside as I passed it, and there was Mrs Sinclair sitting huddled in a chair, staring out at me, her eyes blind with waiting.

She sprang to her feet and called me. 'Mr Hand, please!' I went to her.

'Please close the door!' I closed it and she stood in front of me, trembling, wrenching her hands apart and threading the fingers up again, as though her hands were bound together with invisible string.

'Mr Hand, you're the only one I can talk to. I'm half out of my mind!'

The poor woman's doughy face quivered and twitched as all her natural reticence struggled to master her fear. Something had happened that was forcing her to act in a way she had never acted before in her life, and it was this, the way she was about to act, that horrified her more than the thing that impelled her. She put her head down into her hands and broke into a retching sob.

The sight of her misery calmed me. It was milder to

me than my own thoughts. Reality could not keep distance with my imagination. I looked at her and thought, Stupid woman! Why are you crying? Nothing has happened. You are alive. You can feel your own forehead with your fingertips. You're ugly and old. No one wants you. You might have some cause for terror if you were young and beautiful!

She tried to gasp out her trouble. 'Mr Hand, this terrible murder, the police came for Derek! They've taken him away!'

I put my hand on her shoulder. I was surprised to feel the life running in her under my fingers. There was plenty of life in her, all pent up, but strong and turbulent. I made her sit down. I did all that was required of me. I was comforting and kind. People have always trusted me and turned to me in trouble. I have the right kind of face – nondescript and gentle. I am the sort of person from whom people automatically expect compassion, if nothing else.

I said, 'I'm sure there's some mistake. Perhaps they just want to question him.'

'No, no!' she wailed. 'There's no mistake. We have a cottage in the country. Derek likes to go down there for weekends. I don't go very often. I haven't been for months. Sometimes in spring. Both of us can't get away. Someone has to see to everything here. I don't mind. He enjoys his golf,' she confided with the utmost gravity. 'He's led a very active life, and he gets low-spirited if he doesn't get enough exercise.' Suddenly she remembered what she had been going to tell me, and again she started to tremble. 'They found this girl, in our cottage, at the bottom of the well.'

'Mrs Sinclair, that doesn't mean that your husband

had anything to do with it. The place is empty during the week. Someone, the murderer, could have seen the empty cottage. No one about, quite a good place to hide a body. Or someone that he took there one day might have come, some guest or friend.'

She snatched at my words hungrily. 'It's empty during the week,' she said. 'Yes, it's empty.' Then she remembered something else. 'Mr Hand, the murdered girl, she used to live here in number eight. That Indian girl, she had Miss Sacksena's room. She was with us for quite a long time, and then she went away. They asked Derek, "Do you know this girl?" Of course he knew her! We all knew her.'

'Exactly. That's what I'm saying. You all knew her. I expect they're just asking him questions.'

'It's five weeks, they think; it must have been just after she left, and nobody had reported her missing. She was alone, just a student, studying something. I don't know, I think she was studying interior decoration, but not very seriously. I think she liked to have a good time. She was very pretty and very sophisticated. Not like Miss Sacksena. She went to Birmingham. Only the other day Miss Sacksena said, "Usher hasn't answered my letter yet. Isn't she a naughty girl? She's not much good at writing letters. I suppose she's gadding about".' She broke down again and sobbed. 'Mr Hand, I always knew Derek took girls down there, only I didn't say anything. He's younger than I am. I'm not very well. He needs an outlet . . . a strong, healthy man . . .'

She was convinced that Sinclair had killed the girl. It was a deed that apparently fitted comfortably into her idea of his character. Yet it shocked her. Perhaps what shocked her was her conscious recognition of what he was. A murderer. I wondered if when he came back, exonerated or not, she would leave him and go off and lead her own life.

I tried to comfort her. I told her that they only wanted him for questioning, that they were after someone else. And she didn't believe a word. He was a murderer. Why not? He had murdered her already a dozen times.

I was thinking that they must have taken Sinclair in while I was still talking to Heath and Cunningham, and that now they would be asking him about Doyle. The net was closing in, and Doyle's hours were numbered. And so were hers. If they had not already been counted out.

Upstairs I found Miss Sacksena, also in an emotional state, but accepting death as part of life and therefore not a subject for exceptional dismay. She also seemed attuned to the idea that dreadful and ugly things could happen, not only to other people, but to people one has known and loved, even to oneself.

Looking into her big, heavy-lidded eyes I saw no extension of understanding, no augmentation of horror. What had happened to her little friend Ushar was something that had always been possible, always threatening.

'She was so cheerful', Mr Hand,' she told me. 'I used to say to her, 'Ushar, why are you so cheery? There is not a great deal to be happy about.' What do you think, Mr Hand, is there a great deal in life to be happy about?'

'Not a great deal.'

We were sitting in her room, huddled over the gas fire. She wore a dark silk sari and a blue dressing-gown over it.

Over all that, a red Shetland shawl. She shivered and said, 'It is becoming very cold. Didn't you notice how much colder it was today?'

CHAPTER 16

The next day – it was the last day. There's not much more.

I didn't see Sinclair, though he must have been back. His door was closed as though it might never open again. What was going on in there? I didn't want to think or imagine. Truly, they were the indecent ones.

I spent the morning as I had spent the previous two mornings, looking for Gladys. Tramping the pavements, peering into the shops, drinking in the hissing coffee bars.

But I was repeating actions that had become mechanical, because there was nothing else to do and time had to be used up. It is possible that I actually saw Gladys somewhere that morning. I might have passed her in the street or sat near her in a restaurant having my lunch. I might not have recognised her.

At about four o'clock I found myself outside the Museum, walking up the steps. I was going back to the Print Room. I pushed through the turnstile, past the counter where they sold postcards and Museum publications and straight ahead through the main hall. At the end I came to a barrier, a new one that had been put up since the day before and which meant that instead of turning left through the Indian section, down to the Italian Renaissance, I would have to turn right through the Gothic world and Germany.

The sight of that barrier affected me strangely. I felt as if this alteration to my customary route had been done expressly to torment me and, as I stalked off through the grim, sad litter of the Germanic mind, I kept thinking of the Italian rooms, the gentle marble Madonnas and the shining della Robbia altar pieces. The thought came to me that life had turned against me and forced me out of the way of my inclination.

You'll laugh to hear this, but it seemed to me to be the most cruel blow the fates had dealt me since Rachel's death. And, unlike that supreme disaster, it was petty, malicious, the act of a sadistic god.

I felt that it was useless for me to attempt to do anything. All my acts would end in futility. Useless for me to look for anyone – whoever I sought would evade me. Useless to love – whoever I loved would despise me. Or if I ever won love, my love would die and leave me.

Even so, I began to hope again, even as I came out into the Italian rooms and saw the lovely dimpled boy playing on his blue bagpipes and, above, the light shining through the stained glass window and lying on the stairs in bronze and azure splashes. It wasn't much to hope for. I didn't even realise that I was hoping for anything at all. I simply thought to myself that I would be glad to see Myra again.

I walked through the galleries where they were getting ready for another exhibition and reached the Print Room door. She was inside, packing up her things. She was wearing her green stockings and her chunky black sweater, and standing up and leaning over, so that her lank black hair swept down over her cheeks and the wire necklace with the smooth pebbles fell forward from her flat chest. She turned around, holding her books against her, and I looked into her rugged face with its fiery eyes and splendid Semite nose. She smiled, hugging her feeble drawings.

'Well, you're a bit late. You've only got half an hour.'

What had I come for? To wait in the Print Room for Gladys. If she needed help she'd turn to me. Perhaps she had no one else to turn to and, in any case, I was the man women looked to for help. Mrs Sinclair thought so.

Doyle might look for me too. Suddenly he might think to himself, I do not understand what I am. But I know someone who can tell me.

So I went to the Print Room to wait for them there.

Only when I got there it seemed to me that I had gone for another reason. Myra and I left the Print Room together and walked out, side by side.

I have told you that I felt a longing to confide in her. This feeling no longer troubled me. I felt I had already told her and, if I hadn't, that she didn't need to know. With her I felt secure and at peace.

I asked her if she would like a cup of tea, and we went to the place where Doyle and I had had lunch and sat on the high stools by the counter.

What did we talk about? We talked about art! About Japanese colour prints and their influence on western painting, and about the difficulties of making a living if you were an artist. The copy work she was doing was a job that had come her way. It was nearly finished now. She needed the money. Then she'd go back to the real thing. She was a serious painter – a very bad one. But she didn't know that. She thought she was good. Perhaps one day she will be good, though I doubt it. You only had to listen to her; you only had to look at her alive eyes and her splendid, big mobile features to see that all she was was already expressed. There was nothing left for the pencil or the brush. Only the last feeble vibration of a spirit already expended. I am the kind of man who might make an artist, for all that I am remains unspent within me.

I was glad to be with her. For half an hour I almost forgot my grief for the already dead and the dead to be. We argued about painters and plays. We didn't agree on anything. She was cranky and intolerant. Ideas stood about in her mind in big, undigested lumps. When she expressed them, they sounded splendid. They lit up like torches, but they were quite unrelated to one another. Sometimes they were one another's opposite. She was a woman that you could go on talking to for the rest of your life.

I didn't notice time passing. When we went into the café, it was day outside, and going in the door we entered an interior where we could be private and alone. But slowly we became public, sitting exhibited in a bright electric box, and privacy slipped outside into the darkening street.

She said that she wanted to show me some of her drawings. I didn't want to look at them, but she opened a folder and spread it out on her knees.

I said, 'I'm not going to tell you what I think of them. I wouldn't take the responsibility.'

She said, 'Why not? You are a timid man.'

'Because I would have to tell the truth, and if I said that I believed you had no talent I might help to destroy some talent you had, that I couldn't see, that doesn't show for me in your drawings. If on the other hand I said I thought they were good, I might be applauding some easy, flashy style you have adopted, which is your weakness, your enemy. You must believe in yourself.'

'I do believe in myself. And I don't care what you say. My drawings are no good, but one day they will be. One day I shall find my way of expressing myself. I am still finding my style. I am just getting a hint of it.'

She had tried just about every style. And to me it all looked derivative. I honestly could not detect any hint of talent anywhere. Just an easy facility. She could copy anything.

She was best at portraiture. I didn't know her subjects, of course, but something told me they were very good likenesses. Only the face was always a little weakened. Nothing added, and something taken away.

I felt that her deepest knowledge of the people she had sketched had already been expressed, over cups of coffee perhaps, talking as we were talking now. She had an intense, passionate interest in them as fragments of life that had touched her own. She loved life, and all true artists must hate life a little, turning from it to the manufacture of something more noble and more orderly.

'This boy,' she said, 'he's a German Jew. Isn't that a nervous, interesting face? So nice, but so suspicious. If he lost his handkerchief, he'd accuse you of taking it. He couldn't accept little cruelties, little dishonesties. If you pocketed his box of matches it'd be just as if you'd cheated him of a hundred pounds. I'm sure he'll die in a year or two. He can't possibly survive.'

I wondered if one day she might do a drawing of me, if now, as she looked up with her sharp black eyes, she was engraving my features on her mind to be reproduced later, enfeebled, debilitated . . . Something less than myself as she now saw me.

'And this girl . . .' She turned the page.

And there, looking up at me, was Gladys.

'A difficult subject,' she told me. 'I said to myself when I did it that it was a face without anything to grasp, nothing to stress, you understand. I set myself to do it as a kind of exercise. They are the hardest of all, those soft, unformed kinds of faces. Looking at her you wouldn't have any idea would you, what would happen to that face when she grew older.'

When she grew older! She would not grow old.

'When I do a portrait I look at my subject and say to myself, What will his or her face be like in twenty years' time. And that's the face I draw. Then I reduce it and lift the years off.'

I said, 'You reduce too far, that's the trouble. They are all too young. What you see in them is there, but you're too lenient. You don't make your statement emphatic enough.'

'Do you think so?' She looked up at me. 'I'm so afraid of caricature. It's the easiest thing on earth for me to caricature people, and I'm always trying to avoid it. Perhaps I go too far . . .' She broke off. 'Are you all right? You look awful. You're as white as a sheet.'

'I'm all right. I feel faint, that is . . . That girl . . .' I said the words softly. I barely heard my own voice. And it seemed to me that she had come to me to haunt me. I had lost her for half an hour, and then, like a spectre, she had returned and plucked my sleeve.

I felt no great exultation, for I was certain she was dead. I thought, Well, I must get it over with. I must see the thing through to the end.

What did I mean by that? I can see the question in your eyes. I simply meant that I would follow the trail until I found her murdered body. That there I would face Doyle.

What would I do then? Hand him over to the police, I suppose. And what more? I think I would question him. Yes, there were some questions I would like to ask.

I said, 'When did you do that drawing? The last one you showed me.'

'When? A few weeks ago. I don't exactly remember.'

'And that girl . . .'

'We live in the same boarding-house. She has the room just below mine. Don't tell me she's that girl you keep asking about?'

She gave me a quick, curious look, but asked no more questions. In her world the individual's privacy is sacred. And so is the individual's right to like what he likes, however inferior; to follow his own destiny, wherever it might lead him; to be what he is.

And no matter what I was – madman, idiot, saint – to be what I was was my sacred right, and not to be interfered with. She alone, of all the people I know, has accorded me this privilege.

I asked her for her address and, knowing that I wanted so that I could find Gladys, she gave it to me.

I said, 'Is she a friend of yours?'

'Of mine?' She shook her head. 'What would I have in common with her? She hasn't got a thought in her head but food and cinemas. And men.'

'Then do you love people for their thoughts?'

'Yes,' she said. 'Do you know of a better reason?'

I kept talking to her, knowing all the time that I ought to be hurrying away on my search. But I clung to her still, calming myself in her calm. Mustering my strength.

I said, 'What's her name?'

'You don't even know that?' It was an expression of surprise, tinged with admiration, for the eccentricity of my relationship with Gladys. 'Her name's Gladys Simpson.'

'She told me it was Gladys Wilson.'

'Then she's lying. Either to you or me and a lot of other people. Why would she have to tell lies?'

In her view it was the first step away from being uninteresting that Gladys had made. I read her thought, and I said, 'She isn't an ordinary girl. You're making a mistake if that's what you're thinking. Someone's going to murder her shortly, if this hasn't been done already.'

She turned and fixed me with her eyes, and her face was like the face of a stone carving. For several moments she was silent; then she said, 'You look very ill. You are very pale. I have enjoyed this afternoon. I feel we are friends. I hope you feel it too. I hope we meet again.'

I said, 'I have to go now.'

As I turned to the door she put her hand on my arm and repeated, 'I hope we meet again.'

CHAPTER 17

By now it was dark outside. The address she had given me was in a street off Earl's Court Road. I walked to South Kensington station and took the tube to Earl's Court.

Why didn't I go to the police? It never occurred to me. Now I knew where Gladys lived, where I would find her, if she was alive to be found. To me it was logical that I should be the one to look for her.

Couldn't the police have handled it better? Yes, I suppose they could. I wasn't thinking about handling anything, for better or for worse.

Wasn't I afraid of Doyle? No, I didn't think about fear. I suppose if I had thought about it at all I would have told myself that what I was doing concerned Gladys, Doyle and myself, in the most personal sense. That's how I would have explained my independent action. But there was another reason. There must have been. I don't have to explain that to you.

Soon I was up again in the lit-up streets, in that part of London which is like a slightly disreputable relation of South Kensington. The same features but with bad blood in it somewhere. The same dress but a little shabbier and not so well pressed. Respectability gone and instead an engaging exuberance. I like these parts of London, these poor relations of the affluent and well bred.

The street where Gladys lived was a narrow, U-shaped lane, with ugly, cropped elms that bristled with bare, unpruned twigs, standing in front of solid Victorian houses, all let as bedsitting-rooms and flats. Room to let. Flat to let. There were different people in the streets. I passed a black woman with thin, spindly legs sticking out under a fawn overcoat and a head like a Benin bronze.

Number twelve. A brick wall with cement gateposts; a grubby laurel in a square of front garden.

I walked up the steps, and I was curiously calm. The front door was open and I went inside. There I paused and listened. The hall was like a dark, narrow tunnel carved through the centre of the house, doorways leading onto it. The house itself had sunk into a state of grimy dilapidation. Brown skirtings, sallow walls. It was infinitely depressing. Some time long ago someone had decided that the colours of dirt would prevent dirt from showing. Even the linoleum on the floor by its natural hues gave off an impression of filthiness.

In the hall was an umbrella stand and on the wall a mirror covered in little black dots like the specks of enormous flies. Under the mirror hung a notice insisting on weekly cash terms, and beneath that another notice saying that dogs were not allowed. This command was clearly disregarded, for from up the stairs came the sound of three or four – perhaps more – dogs yapping incessantly. Little grubby, hairy dogs – I could imagine them. There were also the sounds of someone talking in a loud voice, and of radios.

Am I dwelling too long on the unimportant? It all seemed important to me. I had arrived, and felt the advantage of pausing and waiting. Looking about me, listening, I felt an extraordinary perceptiveness, that if I were to put out my hand and touch the notices on the wall, or the gummy brown paint on the skirting boards, my skin would bristle. Little electric charges were reaching out to me from the floors and walls and entering my body like knowledge, speaking to me, telling me what was above and within.

A door opened at the end of the passage and a woman came out, smoking a cigarette and holding a tray of tea things. The cigarette dangled on the corner of her mouth, and she held her head on one side to keep the smoke from her eyes. A good-looking woman past forty, with blue eyes and blonde hair. Hard-faced, hard living.

I said I wanted to see Gladys Simpson.

She jerked her head at the stairs. 'Second floor. Door straight ahead of you at the top of the landing.'

And I went on up, passing a notice that said, 'Please switch off the light.'

It was like a dream. I was the actor in the dream and the observer outside it, dreaming a dream in which another man used my thoughts and lived in my body. I came to the first landing and passed the yapping dogs on my left and the radios on my right.

Above me a door slammed, and I heard a heavy, precipitant step. At the turn of the stair Doyle came into view, careering down with his hand on the banister.

When he saw me, he stopped, gasped and fell back against the wall. His hands hung down limp at his sides in that curious, slack way that I had noticed before. He, also, was like a man dreaming another man's dream. I thought that I knew exactly why he was there, where he had been, where he was going. Only, of course, I didn't know.

I said, 'What have you done to her, Doyle?'

He didn't answer me. He stood there, leaning on the wall with his slack, outward hanging arms, looking at me out of his dark, pearly eyes.

I suppose by then he must have been in a sweat of terror. It cleansed his face, erasing all the handsome bestiality that I had so detested. He looked calm, you might say spiritual.

But I didn't have much time to enjoy this new appearance of saintliness, for he launched himself upon me, and if I hadn't stepped aside we would have gone crashing down together. He gripped the banister to keep his balance as he passed me. And I saw his face close to mine; saw the clots in his eyes and heard the hiss of his terror. Turning at the bottom of the landing, he gave me a quick, appalled glance and then went hurtling on, down the next flight of stairs to the hall and out to the front door.

I suppose he expected me to follow him. He must have known by then he was a hunted man – for what he had done in the past if not for what he had done now. But I just stood watching him go. I thought, The police can deal with him, which they did, as you know. He crashed out of the front door and collided into the man who had been following me. And when he knocked him down and careered off there were the two men in the car to give chase.

They knew then, finally and for certain, that there was a Doyle, and he kept them busy for half an hour or so.

It was very quiet now on the staircase. No, it was not very quiet. Why did I say that? It seemed so quiet for a moment that I felt I could hear the voice of my own thoughts. But there was an awful racket going on. The dogs yapping, those radios blaring away. They would not have stopped just for me.

Slowly I turned and walked to the top of the landing. My feet were like stones. I could hardly lift them. There, ahead of me, was the closed door to Gladys's room. I stopped before it, but I did not open it.

I am telling you what I felt exactly – the appalling suspense, the sense of weight in my feet. My heart seemed to beat beyond the power of my body to contain it. It seemed to me that the frame of my ribs was breaking apart. But why, you are asking me. You want me to analyse these curious physical sensations and give you some answer, is that it? You want me to say that it was fear of what I might find – the murdered girl behind the door – dread of my discovery, hope for the thin thread of probability that still attached her to life. I cannot say. Well, I can't lie to you, can I? Isn't that your job – detecting lies?

I don't know. That's what I'm going to tell you. This, I fully realise, is an important moment. It's where you being to look for causes, isn't it? But I can't help you. I'm sorry. It's no use.

There is a point when all emotion loses its identity and becomes the same. When joy is fear and terror is desire. When love is hate and sorrow is ecstasy. Just as there is a point when all colours are one. When blue, green and red are a blaze of light.

I can't even tell you how long I stood there in this brimming state of emotion. Then I put out my hand and touched the door handle. This brought me to myself a little. The round, brass knob, I remember, wobbled slightly in its socket and, very quietly, so as not to wake the dead, I opened the door.

She was kneeling on the floor. In front of her she had a paper pattern pinned to a piece of green cloth, and she was cutting it with a pair of long shining scissors. She was wearing tight, tartan slacks and a red sweater, and her black hair, which hung loose around her head, fell down her back and over her shoulders in silky undulations.

She looked up at me, and her big, pink lips drooped open. 'Good heavens! Mr Hand . . .'

'Gladys!' I said to her. 'Gladys!' I stumbled across the room and groped for a chair. My legs would hardly hold me.

I can tell you what I felt now. Oh, yes! I can tell you that! I felt that the world had dropped away under my feet. I had been certain she would be dead. Certain! And here was this plump, breathing, living substitute for the tragedy I had expected. I was disappointed.

Well, isn't that natural? You don't think so? I feel myself that it's perfectly natural, but that not many men would admit it. But I have to admit it, don't I? What would be the use of telling you that I felt a great rush of relief? Of course I did. But it was small, it was puny, compared to the great rush of disappointment. There is a grandeur about any supreme disaster, a splendour that entices us. I know. I learned all about suffering when Rachel died. I have never before or since known anything so voluptuous, so exquisite as that suffering. It made me mad, and in the end I'd rather be mad than sane.

It is, I concede, quite horrible for any normal man to be disappointed by the unexpected safety of his imperilled love and, as soon as I knew that I was disappointed, I was so horrified I became faint and cold all over. I shouted, mumbled and sighed out all the best and most conventional feelings.

'Gladys, thank God you're safe! I've been out of my mind! Thank God!'

'Of course I'm safe. What are you going on about?' She was sitting back on her haunches looking up at me, and the pair of scissors lay opened out like a silver cross on the green cloth before her. I noticed that she was too fat to wear slacks. Her thighs seemed to be bursting out of them and her breasts out of the red sweater.

I went on insisting on all my correct and conventional feelings. 'I saw him on the stairs,' I said. 'Thank God, you're safe. I thought . . . '

'Who? Freddy? I don't know what got into him. He was looking out of the window, and then suddenly he dashed off like mad. He'll get over it.'

'What? What will he get over? Tell me!' I was half frantic, shouting, gasping, working myself up into a fever of relief and concern. And all the time it grew more difficult. All the time that cold, shrivelled sense of disappointment grew like winter in my heart.

'We had a row. What's the matter with you, Mr Hand? You look awful! You're as white as anything.'

'He didn't hurt you! Tell me he didn't hurt you!'

Springing from my chair I sank down on my knees beside her. I seized her hands and clasped them hard in my own. Hard, hard. Crushing the little plump hands – sticky and warm.

She tried to pull them away from me, but I kept holding them. I saw her soft, rounded face close to my own. The big lips and the soft, silky hair springing up from her temples and behind her ears.

'Freddy hurt me? He's very fond of me. He wouldn't hurt a hair on my head.'

I said, 'The people we love are often the ones we want to hurt.'

I tugged at her hands, and now her face was so close to mine her features were big and blurred. At that distance – the intimate position for crime and love – all expression goes out of a face, and it looks blank and unearthly.

'Please let me go, Mr Hand. You're hurting me!'

'I wouldn't hurt a hair on your head!'

I dropped her hands and gripped her head in my fingers, holding it by handfuls of hair, gripping her hair behind the ears on either side of her head and holding her to me by the ropes of her hair. 'I'll look after you! I'll protect you! Trust me!

I don't know what I said. Something like that. Words poured out of me. Passionate, imploring words. I told her I loved her. I told her that I'd protect her from danger and look after her and cherish her. She would have nothing to fear from me. I'd be tender and kind to her. I'd protect her from Doyle.

And all the time, as this hot flow of words poured from my lips, there was a part of my mind that stood aside, that was cool and still and engendered its own thoughts. And this part of me was thinking that Rachel, my wife, had drowned in green water. Dead and gone. Rachel who had never known I loved her and had never asked to be loved. And that Gladys was alive. The fat, stupid, silly little bitch.

'Let me go, Mr Hand, let me go!'

Putting her hands on my chest, she tried to thrust her body away from me, leaning back in my arms and straining her head away from me, shaking it from side to side to unloose my clasp.

'Don't do that, Gladys,' I said to her softly.

I remember that. For now I am reaching the end of my recollection, and the moment before the dark is very bright. 'Don't do that.'

But she only strained back more and struggled more fiercely. Silly bitch, seductive and stupid. She was asking for some man to get annoyed with her.

'Don't do that!'

'I couldn't, Mr Hand! Not with you. I don't like you ! Not like that! Let me go!'

Now you will have to allow of some vagueness. For my memory begins to divide like a river at its delta. What I said, what I ought to have said, what I might have said . . . A river at its delta, with the vast vacant sea beyond. There is some understandable difficulty. I suppose the shock surges back and breaks upon the past.

I remember then that she got away. Only we were still on the floor; then she tried to get up. And that I lunged forward, falling with my hands on the green cloth and grabbed her by the legs and brought her down. I have the impression that I struck my head. Something seems to be needed to account for the complete cessation of my consciousness. In any case I can't help you. I've thought, of course. Don't imagine I haven't. I want to remember.

There must have been five minutes or so for which no one can account because no one was there.

Then you've got plenty of witnesses. Four of them, wasn't it? The two policemen, that woman I met downstairs, and another woman who lived in the room with the yapping dogs.

They'll tell you how they heard her screams and came rushing up and broke in the door. And how they found me there, sitting quietly, so they say, with my murdered girl. And the scissors, and all the hair.

They let me keep the hair for a while because I wept and became frantic when they tried to take it away from me. Otherwise I was perfectly quiet. Apparently when they asked me why I did it I replied that she didn't like me. Only that wasn't the reason, was it? What was the reason? You are supposed to know. In any case, I must have been insane. Well, I was, wasn't I? The law says so.

And what does the law say now? I am still here in this antiseptic cell. Only I have outgrown it. I shouldn't be here, should I? It is all bogus. We both know that I am as sane as any man, and that there are circumstances in which every man will penetrate so deeply into labyrinths of love or grief or pain that any talk of sanity or insanity is meaningless.

It is all over now. It will never happen again. I have had my day. I have made my protest. Now, once again, I am a feeble, craven man. I have even ceased to grieve for my dead wife. She has gone, submerged in the past, a ripple in green water.

Myra comes to see me every week – it was kind of you to allow that. Part of my rehabilitation, I suppose, and very effective. She has told me that I am the most interesting man she has ever met. The most completely 'myself'. I even murder when I feel like it.

I know that if I ever get out of here she will possess me. And I could do worse. The future contains some hope for me, and I condition my timid, guilty mind to face it with anticipation. So when I think of a woman at all, I think of Myra, my splendid Hittite girl, with her beautiful nose and her stirring conversation, not of those other two . . . the girl I killed and my wife who was killed by the sea.

As for Doyle, I think so little of Doyle, I feel so hazy about him, I begin to wonder if he might not have been a figment of my imagination.

No? You are certain? Well, that's good. I'm pleased there's a Doyle.

But what you really want to know is do I feel any guilt for the death of that poor, silly girl? Have I repented my crime? I must repent, mustn't I, before you can feel sure of me. Sure enough to let me loose again into the world where guilt is a necessity of existence.

Of course, of course. Rest assured.

Myra says I must not repent. That the only real crime is the crime against one's own nature. And that mine is fulfilled. That I was as I was and I am as I am. She thinks a lot of me. She has given up drawing anyone else, and even I feel bound to admit that she has discovered some striking possibilities in my face.

I am afraid she is drawing the past. She is drawing the man who waited in the Print Room for Gladys and Doyle. The man who sat talking to her in the café with the red Formica tables.

Those days are gone, and I am an ordinary puny human being. Not the man she knew. She loves me, she tells me. I wonder when she will wake from her illusion. Perhaps never. It is quite possible to nurse an illusion till the end of one's life.

I don't mind living a lie. Indeed, it seems the only reasonable way to live. And I hope she never sees me as I am, for if she does she will certainly leave me. And I need someone to look after me. I am growing old. I am guilty and afraid. I would like a little of that calm, tepid contentment that most human beings call happiness. It is all I will have now, and all I can give. I would like it, and Myra can give it to me.

So let us hope that she continues in her self-deception and sees me forever as I was – the hero, the madman, in the great days of his grief.

AFTERWORD

Charlotte Jay was born Geraldine Mary Jay in 1919 in Adelaide. She grew up in Adelaide, attending Girton School (now Pembroke School) and the University of Adelaide. She worked as a secretary in Adelaide, Sydney, Melbourne and London during the 1940s and as a court stenographer for the (Australian) Court of Papua New Guinea during 1949. During the 1950s she and her husband, John, who worked for unesco, travelled and lived in Lebanon, Pakistan, Thailand, India and France. They operated an oriental art business in Somerset between 1958 and 1971, and since then, in Adelaide until she died in 1996. (John died in 1982.)

Charlotte Jay was the name she used to publish most of her nine mystery novels. Except for *The Voice of the Crab* (1974), they were first published between 1951 and 1964 and reflect a life spent travelling and her fascination with local cultures and ethnological questions, as do her six 'straight' novels published as Geraldine Halls between 1956 and 1982. Only her first novel, *The Knife is Feminine*, is set in Australia. In others, the action takes place in Pakistan, Japan, Thailand, England, Lebanon, India, Papua New Guinea, and the Trobrian Islands. Most of her Charlotte Jay mysteries were first published by Collins in London and Harper in New York. They have appeared in various editions and have been translated around the world – *The Fugitive Eye* was made into a Hollywood movie starring Charlton Heston – but have not until now been published in Australia. She confessed she became rather confused about her national identity during her heyday as a mystery writer. The American reviewers always referred to her as British, the British reviewers called her an Australian, and the Australian reviewers more or less ignored her. Something of Charlotte Jay's mixed identity might be reflected in Sarah Lane, the heroine of *Arms for Adonis*, a young British woman who 'felt she had been born in the wrong country and craved the sun'.

She had described her motives and methods as a mystery writer like this: 'I began writing mystery stories largely because of my delight in the novels of Wilkie Collins and Le Fanu and the stories of Poe. I read these books with terror and fascination when I was quite young and their influence can be seen in several of my early novels. When my first books were published most of the crime stories at that time were written by skilled writers of crime and detection, usually with a well-born ex-Oxford or Cambridge amateur as the private detective as the central character, appearing in the manner of the Scarlet Pimpernel, something of a fool, but omniscient and strides ahead of the reader. In America the same fashion prevailed along with crime stories following in the tradition of Dashiell Hammett and Raymond Chandler. I knew I could not compete with excellent exponents of these varied trends. Many had direct experience of police procedure which I did not feel confident of learning anything much about. And indeed I felt no interest in doing so. I set out to frighten my readers by asking them to identify themselves with a character battling for survival in a lonely, claustrophobic situation. My publishers on several occasions demanded that, in the interest of logicality, my threatened character should call the police. I always contested their suggestions and sometimes rewrote whole chapters to accommodate my conviction that my characters must stumble on alone and unaided through their private nightmares.' (From *Twentieth Century Crime and Mystery Writers*, St James Press, 1985).

Arms for Adonis was first published in 1961 by Collins (UK) and Harper (USA) and in 1962 as a paperback Collier Mystery Classic. Charlotte Jay had revised and in places rewritten the novel for publication in Wakefield Crime Classics. She wrote the book during the months leading up to the invasion of Egypt in 1956 by England, France and Israel (the Suez Crisis). She was living in Beirut during a one year 'tour of duty' by her husband, John, who was a senior official for the United Nations Relief and Works Agency in the Middle East. Her time was spent immersed in the history and atmosphere of Lebanon, a country she loved in a period of great happiness in her own life.

This tranquil, yet intense awareness is vividly and beautifully reflected in the sensual description of landscape. One of Charlotte Jay's skills was to give a scene, a setting, a country, a living presence (as in the evocations of jungle in *Beat Not the Bones*, Wakefield Crime Classics, 1992). Beirut and Lebanon are both minor protagonists in *Arms for Adonis*. Odd moments, snapshots, cameo portraits fill the opening chapter and they variously allow the reader to 'touch', 'smell', 'see' Beirut.

Later, the country's interior comes to life:

The broad green valley stretched away to north and south, and in front of them, surprisingly near, the long range of the Lebanon rose up like a barrier. These are extraordinary mountains, appearing from over the Beka'a both massive and delicate, their lower slopes intricately folded and pierced by innumerable valleys, their crests glittering with snow – not the abundant whiteness of winter, this had melted away – but summer snow like veins of silver struck down between the naked grey ridges.

The lower slopes were warm with sunshine; rocks and stones shone blinding white in the thin, clear air and almond and peach trees putting out new leaf trembled and shimmered as though green water was netted in their branches. But as they mounted higher the mood of the landscape became sad and threatening; huge ash-grey clouds moved swiftly down the mountain slopes blotting out the road ahead.

As they went higher, the mist thickened. The posts at the side of the road, grey boulders, thorn bushes, and almond trees black and twisted like corroded iron, appeared like spectres. A shepherd in a white keffiyeh and baggy trousers stood watching over them, a ghostly figure with the mist whirling around him.

These random instances represent Charlotte Jay's cre-
ative method in this book – the overwhelming use of the
metaphorical trope of light and white, sometimes daz-
zlingly so. The device is brilliant and justified, because
the story revolves around the Greek myth of Venus and
Adonis (the Romans 'claimed' Venus as Aphrodite). The
myth links the political thriller and the love strands of the
story – Colonel Ahmed is Adonis; Sarah, Aphrodite. Alert
readers should have picked the inevitability of their union
for they were destined for one another. As Charlotte Jay
commented in conversation with the editors, 'You cannot
step out of a myth.' And why the Adonis myth? Charlotte
Jay explains: 'Adonis is very important in Lebanon. You see,
the Adonis river rises in Lebanon . . . although it is a Greek
myth, somehow or other, Lebanon seems to have taken it
to itself. You have the source of the Adonis and then about
ten miles away, over the top of the mountains, there is a
lake and it's said that the pilgrims from the Adonis festivals
practised fertility rites when the males severed their penises
and walked along the ancient Emperor Domitian's Road
and threw themselves into the lake for purification.'

This aspect of Lebanon's mythic past is joltingly
described in Sarah's vision during her escape from Äin
Houssaine.

Arms for Adonis has been classed as a brilliant travel
book – 'excellent scenery and local colour' (*Saturday
Review*) and, tragically, it could be so read. 'Tragically'
because Jay's Beirut and Lebanon no longer exist. (As we
write this afterword in 1993, the Israeli army bombs the
civilian population of Southern Lebanon.) Her lovely

evocations represent lost journeys. Obviously, this travelogue view is only partly accurate. There are more important emphases.

The political aspect of the book needs no development here other than to point out Jay's sanity in her depictions of the crazy fluctuations and alliances in the Middle East. Her method is that of the skilled novelist, allowing her characters *in situ* to comment on the larger actualities, often with a wry, ironic humour. Much of the blame for every problem, then, was targeted at Britain, the cynical diplomatic manipulations of America and France being unremarked for the most part. Jay put it neatly: 'in the Middle East . . . so much that was distressing to the humanitarian mind – the refugee camps in the Jordan valley, the devastated areas of Jerusalem where Jew had murdered Arab and Arab had murdered Jew, even purdah, beggars and the suspicions of the Syrian customs officials – could, if one felt so inclined, be laid at the door of British imperialism.' Britain has gone, but the wild switches of policy and emotions are no different now from what they were forty years ago. Jay offers, however, a civilised, if wistful, solution to the chaos, one utterly devoid of political and international correctness and, therefore, likely to be derided by the mad political leaders of our era.

In the final analysis the book is about marriages, comings together, workable assimilations. Sarah's name is both Jewish and Muslim; St Joseph's Maronite church 'seems to embody the pagan temple, the mosque and the church – an oriental and Mediterranean synthesis'; Sarah (an Englishwoman) realises a 'mysterious and frightening accord that was between them' (between herself and Raschid Ahmed, a Syrian); Jay says of Beirut that 'it is both European and Asian and must perforce face both ways – or, at any rate, it cannot afford to alarm its own divided nature by looking too fixedly in one direction'.

These compromises are themselves part of the 'mystery' of the book, in which shifting commitments and liaisons represent the political and personal realities in a fictional and actual world which has no apparent fixed centre. That descriptions of the chaos can still satisfy the reader is a reflection of Charlotte Jay's skill and romantic optimism, probably the only sensible resolution of a story set in a strange and mad time.

Peter Moss and Michael J. Tolley, general editors of the Wakefield Crime Classics series, were colleagues at the University of Adelaide. Late in 1988, they began assembling a series of Australian 'classic' crime fiction and soon realised that the problem was not going to be one of finding sufficient works of high quality, but of finding a bold enough publisher fired with the same vision.

Also available in

WAKEFIELD CRIME CLASSICS

BEAT NOT THE BONES
by Charlotte Jay

People changed; they were no longer recognisable as Australians. Frustrations and misfortunes festered into wounds here, deranged the mind and poisoned the blood.

Suicide, or murder? Newly arrived in Papua, where even the luscious vegetation conspires with the bureaucrats to bewilder her, Stella Warwick is determined to prove her husband did not take his own life. Defying the patronising concern of officials, she ventures deep into the jungle, striding ever closer to the horrifying heart of the mystery.

'This might easily scare you out of your wits. Extremely well-handled mystery, authentic horror and atmosphere that closes in like jungle heat.'

L.G. Offord, *San Francisco Chronicle*

'A unique and powerful experience in mystery/suspense writing by one of the most important writers of far off places and their mysterious qualities.'

Dorothy B. Hughes, *Twentieth Century Crime and Mystery Writers*

'A superb novel ... a wonderfully crafted crime story ... full of suspense, its episodes artfully juxtaposed now to provide shock, now black comedy, now anguished bewilderment.'

David Smith, *Body Dabbler*

ARMS FOR ADONIS
by Charlotte Jay

The blood of Adonis, thought Sarah, remembering the church that was built like a pagan temple. Coquelicot rouge – the symbol of a dying man whose blood stained the hillside in the spring.

Sarah Lane, abandoning her French lover for the brilliant Lebanese sunshine, believes that the day will belong to her alone. But when a street bomb hurls her into the arms of a dangerously handsome Syrian colonel, she finds herself trapped once again. Is this a kidnapping? A seduction? Or merely the chaos of the Middle-East?

'Charlotte Jay cannot write a dull or graceless sentence. The heroine of *Arms for Adonis*, Sarah Lane, is fascinatingly alive, and her convincing adventures have a background so vividly depicted that Lebanon itself becomes a protagonist in the novel.'
New York Times

'Exciting action and brilliantly evocative description of a kind seldom encountered in a thriller. *Arms for Adonis* is well above average in every way.'
British Book News

'Charlotte Jay's eye for the scene is sharp and so is her eye for the attitudes of human pretension. Wryly romantic and a keen delight.'
New York Herald Tribune

Wakefield Press is an independent publishing and
distribution company based in Adelaide, South Australia.
We love good stories and publish beautiful books.
To see our full range of books, please visit our website at
www.wakefieldpress.com.au
where all titles are available for purchase.
To keep up with our latest releases, news and events,
subscribe to our monthly newsletter.

Find us!

Facebook: www.facebook.com/wakefield.press
Twitter: www.twitter.com/wakefieldpress
Instagram: www.instagram.com/wakefieldpress